*Jack Vance*

# The Dark Ocean

*Jack Vance*

# The
# Dark
# Ocean

*John Holbrook Vance*

Spatterlight Press Signature Series, Volume 20

Published by Spatterlight Press

Cover art by Howard Kistler

ISBN 978-1-61947-141-2

Spatterlight Press LLC

Spatterlight
P R E S S
340 S. Lemon Ave #1916
Walnut, CA 91789

www.jackvance.com

*Jack Vance*
# The Dark Ocean

# Chapter I

## 1

After Panama the voyage became a sunny blue and white dream. The ship slid through the water with a lazy motion; there was every inducement to relax, to ponder, to meditate. As the sparkling days passed, the first part of the voyage began to lose reality, for which Betty Haverhill was grateful. With melancholy amusement she considered herself as she had been only a month before. Innocent, naïve: these were the obvious adjectives. Angry persons had used others: smug, pampered, vain, self-centered — but these were undeserved, unkind half-truths. Betty was deficient in worldly wisdom, and she had been guilty of superficiality, for which much of the blame could be laid to Mother.

Mother's world, and perforce much of Betty's, was restricted to things which were 'nice'. She kept claret and sherry, but very little whiskey; she preferred lobster to steak, Chopin to Bach. For the benefit of her married friends she archly endorsed the principle of a man around the house, but Betty's father had wandered away after two uneasy years, and Mother had never remarried.

They lived in a district of pleasant old homes in Menlo Park, thirty miles south of San Francisco. Mother was not a snob, but class-consciousness was the air she breathed. It simply had never occurred to her that plumbers, garbage-men and the like existed apart from their duties. She saw them fulfilling their roles as an organic necessity, in the same manner that a piano provides music, or a walnut tree bears walnuts. Betty had learned, therefore, to classify people by the most obvious of their aspects. Halfway across the Atlantic, considering this matter, she became vaguely excited, as if a truth of great import hovered at the verge of her mind. Everyone, she thought, moved through life behind a screen of symbols: words, clothes, gestures. It was an essential step in the process of growing up to recognize the symbols for what they were, and to feel behind them for the concealed personality. The applicable word was 'sympathy' in its classic sense, without overtones of pity. 'Tout comprendre, c'est tout pardonner': who wrote that? Voltaire? Surely he was wrong. One could understand selfishness and cruelty without condoning them. Betty wondered if she truly understood these qualities. No, she decided, heaving a sigh. I am more or less normal; there are many sensations I have not yet experienced. Perhaps I still am not completely sophisticated. And if I'm not, I don't want to be. Remembering the Betty Haverhill who had embarked on the *Garda* so short a time ago, she sighed again for her lost girlhood.

Betty's mother, having no inclination toward men, took it for granted that Betty shared her views. By one means or another she arranged that Betty met only the nicest boys of the best families, with the result that Betty, disillusioned with the bumptious young twerps presented to her, skipped the boy-crazy stage and gave very little worry. Mother was encouraged in one of her most cherished ambitions: a medical career for Betty. Betty obligingly struggled through two years of the pre-med curriculum at Stanford, tinkering with ideas and objects she privately felt were far better ignored. At the end of her fourth semester she flunked out of school with great relief.

Mother was shocked by Betty's nonchalance. "I'm absolutely astounded! I had no idea your grades were so bad!"

"Oh come, Mother. You knew all about my midterms."

"But I thought the finals were mainly what counted."

"I made the same grades in my finals."

Mother bit her lips. "In my day we'd consider it a disgrace."

"It's been done before. It'll be done again."

"But you'd so planned on a career! I just can't understand it!"

Betty patted her mother's shoulder. "I'd make a terrible doctor. In the first place, I can't stand the sight of blood."

"There's always psychology, or even research! Think of Doctor Salk, think of the good he's done!"

"The fact remains, they've flunked me out."

Mother said with determination, "You can make up your grades! It's just a matter of having a goal! If you *will* something hard enough, you can do it!"

Betty seated herself in the big green armchair and drew a deep breath. "Actually, Mother, it's all for the best. Something much more exciting has come up. I telephoned Father this morning and told him the news. He wasn't disturbed or even surprised. He didn't think I was cut out to be a doctor either."

"He wouldn't," said Mother scornfully.

Betty's father, a mining engineer who had made a great deal of money from tungsten, then uranium, then half a dozen other things, lived a free-and-easy life in Denver, and represented everything of which Mother disapproved.

"Anyway," Betty added casually, "Father said that if I wanted to travel he'd pay all the expenses — to Europe, around the world, anywhere I wanted to go. Naturally I said I loved the idea."

The two shocks, related but distinct, struck Mother dumb. "That's ridiculous," she said at last.

"Mother! How can you say that! It's wonderful!"

"You're so young, so inexperienced!"

"Not for long. Travel is broadening — you've said so yourself. Now don't let's argue, Mother — because I'm absolutely determined."

Nevertheless, there was argument, until Betty finally lost her temper. She pointed out that she was of age, of sound mind and good character, at liberty to travel to Gehenna, if she felt like it.

Mother sniffed. "What of all your boy friends? What of Ted Bunpole?"

"He's the least of my worries."

"Are you sure?" asked Mother with unaccustomed archness. "I thought that perhaps there was some sort of an understanding."

Betty laughed incredulously. "Who told you that? Ted?"

"I should think he'd be just the kind of boy you'd like. I've known his mother all my life. He's got a good job, a nice car, he played football at college."

Betty looked curiously at her mother. "I believe you'd rather have me marry that pest than to go to Europe."

"Yes, I would, since you seem bent on giving up your career. I really don't see what you have against Ted."

"In the first place," said Betty, "he's a typical young jerk. He's got some ridiculous office job and calls himself a junior executive. He wears a hat. He makes three-fifty a month, he's just bought a new car on which he pays a hundred and fifty. He reads men's magazines. He goes to prize fights. He drinks nothing but Haig and Haig and calls for it in bars. They pour him any old rot-gut and he doesn't know the difference. His idea of living it up is a weekend at Las Vegas. Shall I go on?"

Mother said coldly, "You do Ted a great injustice. He's a perfectly normal young man with a great deal of charm."

"What really clinches it," said Betty, "is the name: Ted Bunpole. When you say it fast it sounds like Bumple. I'd be Mrs. Betty Bumple."

Mother turned away. "You're simply impossible. Go on your trip! If something awful happens, don't expect any sympathy from me."

# 2

Ted Bunpole was also disturbed to learn of Betty's plans. "I don't like this, Betty. Not at all! In fact, I'm against it."

Betty said that, with all the will in the world, she couldn't care less. She was in a bad humor, not improved by the fact that Mother had ostentatiously left them alone in the living room.

Ted had dressed carefully for the occasion, in slacks of a soft smoke-brown corduroy, a shirt of muted green, blue and red tartan, a gray cashmere sweater. He bent forward, took Betty's hands, which Betty snatched away. Ted pretended not to notice. "I've got a wonderful idea. Here's you, here's me: let's get married. Right now. We'll jump in the Merc and be in Reno in no time at all."

"Are you out of your mind? I'm going to Europe. I've already bought my ticket."

Ted compressed his lips. "You're a headstrong little son of a gun."

"I'm nothing of the sort." Betty picked a banana out of the fruit bowl, peeled it. "I just know what I want to do, and I plan to do it."

"Well then," growled Ted, "exactly what are you doing?"

"I'm sailing in about three weeks, on a freighter, from San Francisco to Genoa. The voyage takes over a month. It costs three hundred and eighty-five dollars. There are only twelve passengers. I leave on July 22nd."

"Mmf. And how long are you planning to stay away?"

"As long as I feel like it."

"Mmf." Ted kicked out his legs, slumped deeper into the chair.

"You look the picture of disgust," said Betty through the banana.

"Why shouldn't I be disgusted? I want you to marry me and you go flying off to Europe. You'll probably take up with some long-haired artist, you'll get pregnant and then you'll wonder why good old Ted doesn't show up to make an honest woman out of you."

Betty laughed. "You're just sore that the artist made out where you didn't."

Ted jerked up in his chair, his face blazing with such fury that Betty thought she had carried things too far.

"The trouble with you," croaked Ted, "is that you're spoiled rotten! Darling little Betty. Surrounded by a bunch of females, all cooing and pampering. Your nose runs, one of your aunts brings a handkerchief. You yawn, another aunt holds her hand over your mouth. You go to the bathroom —"

Betty interrupted. "Exactly how am I spoiled? I'm curious."

"You're a snob."

"Because I won't marry you? That's not snobbery, that's good taste. You make three-fifty a month —"

"Three-sixty."

"— three-sixty — so you got a raise. You still spend half of it on that foolish pile of tin and the other half on clothes. You haven't read a book since the Kinsey Report. And you have the nerve to ask me to marry you. You'd stick me in a tract house along the Bayshore Highway, with two TV sets and a pop-up toaster. No, no, Ted Bumple — not for me. There's thousands of girls who'll ride to Reno in your Mercury, and be happy as a pig with you and your TV sets. I may get pregnant by the artist but I'm damned if I'll let myself in for a living death."

There was a pause. Ted rose heavily to his feet. "That's pretty definite. I hope you don't get hurt."

"Hurt? Why should I get hurt?"

Ted shrugged. "Some strange types batting around the world. You're just a kid."

Betty laughed ruefully. "You and Mother: a fine pair of vultures! You'd be glad if something *did* happen to me!"

"Of course not," said Ted in irritation. "I don't wish anyone bad luck." He started for the door, paused. "What's the name of this scow you're going on?"

"The *Garda*, as in Lake Garda."

At the door Ted swung around, turned his smile on Betty. "How about going out tomorrow night? Dinner in the city? Something grand, really fine?"

"No thanks, Ted. In the first place you can't afford it. You have your car payment to make. In the second place, I don't want to argue any more. In the third place — well, never mind; you'd only be mad all over again."

"Please?"

"No."

"Pretty please?"

"Don't tease, Ted."

"Gad! You're a stubborn witch!" cried Ted. He tried to seize Betty, to kiss her into sighing submission, as he had seen it done in the movies, but Betty stepped back and swung the door between them. Ted marched down the walk toward his car, which suddenly he hated.

Betty called after him, "Goodnight, Ted! Drive carefully!"

# CHAPTER II

## 1

THE *GARDA*, A MEDITERRANEAN LINE freighter flying the Italian flag, sailed from San Francisco on the evening of July 22nd, bound for ports in El Salvador, Panama, Venezuela, Spain and Italy. Betty's father could not be on hand, but he had sent a *bon voyage* telegram. Mother, Aunt Ethel and Uncle Graham drove Betty to the dock. Mother had been maddeningly deliberate.

They arrived on the dock an hour before sailing time. Mother was dismayed when she saw the ship. "It's just an old tramp steamer!"

"It's informal," Betty agreed. "That's the charm of freighter travel."

Betty's three best girl friends had been waiting in a car nearby, and with them was Ted Bunpole, uncharacteristically diffident. Everyone climbed the gangway, Uncle Graham and Ted carrying Betty's suitcases. Five or six seamen, swarthy, dirty and rather under-sized, leaned against the rail, watching with unabashed interest.

"They don't seem a very cleanly lot," Mother remarked. "I hope they know their business."

"They brought the ship here," said Betty, "presumably they can take it away again."

"I wish I shared your confidence."

Betty surrendered her ticket and passport to an officious young officer in sun-tans, who she later learned to be the purser. A mess-boy led them along passageways, up two flights of steep steel stairs. Cabin #2 was on the port side of the bridge deck, aft. It contained two neat white beds, each with its reading light and electric fan, a writing desk with a swivel chair, a wash-basin, a medicine cabinet and two clothes closets.

"Very nice," said Aunt Ethel. "As clean as can be!"

Mother could hardly disagree. "Don't forget, always lock your suitcases and your cabin door, or you'll lose everything you own!"

Leaving the cabin, they climbed to the top deck. There were several dozen other people here — passengers and those who had come to see them off. Betty, eagerly looking here and there, was able to pick out a number of her fellow passengers: four Latin-American ladies in pink and green floral prints; a short gray-haired man of sixty; a tall, dark lad of Betty's own age; an intellectual-looking couple.

Ted and Uncle Graham found seats for everyone who wanted to sit. There was half an hour of strained last-minute conversation; then one of the ship's officers came up on deck, passed among the various groups announcing that the ship departed in fifteen minutes. Betty descended with her friends and family to the gangway. Aunt Ethel kissed her, gave her a hug; Uncle Graham pecked at her cheek. Mother gripped both of Betty's hands, her eyes brimming with tears. Betty began to cry, then laughed. "We look so funny; we've got to behave ourselves! Now don't mope while I'm gone."

"I'll try not to," quavered Mother, "I really do hope you'll have a wonderful time. Just be careful — very, very careful!"

"Of course, Mother! Don't worry! Thousands of people travel!"

They kissed each other; Mother turned and descended the gangway.

The lines were thrown off, the ship's whistle blew, a pair of tugs pulled the ship out into the stream.

Betty climbed back up to the top deck, went out on the wing of the flying bridge, waved until the figures on the dock could no longer be seen. She drew a deep breath, infinitely relieved that the farewells were over. Now — to make the acquaintance of the other passengers. Beside her stood the intellectual-looking couple. Alec Cato (so he introduced himself) was in his late forties, wearing a baggy brown tweed jacket and old gray flannel slacks. He had a round pale face, distinguished mainly by heavy black horn-rim glasses, a sparse sprinkle of kinky black hair. His wife, Ora, thin and tough as a smoked herring, was of indeterminate age, with an inquisitive beak of a nose, a crest of rank red hair.

"You're traveling alone?" asked Ora Cato, raking Betty with sharp black eyes.

"Yes," said Betty lamely. She felt a pang of annoyance. There was no reason for her to be on the defensive. "Yes," she said airily. "I'm traveling alone."

She looked around, to appraise the other passengers. To her right stood the Latin-American ladies; beyond, Ted Bunpole leaned against the rail, grinning blandly. He moved around the four Latin-American ladies, joined her.

For a moment Betty could not find her tongue. Then she cried angrily, "What in heaven's name are you doing here?"

"Surprised?" asked Ted.

"Yes," said Betty grimly. "I'm surprised."

"I thought you'd be."

"Do you mind explaining what you're doing here?"

"It's obvious. I'm traveling to Europe. You talked me into it. I sold my car, quit my job, and here I am."

Betty could hardly speak for fury. "I came on this ship to see a few new faces. Now I've got to look at you."

"Your pleasure is flattering."

"It's not pleasure."

"It should be," said Ted. "I'm your boy, just the way you like me. No more expensive car, no more stupefying job. I'm going to be a vagabond musician. We'll roam the highways and byways, you dancing for coppers, me with a red bandana around my head playing the accordion."

Betty looked at him, uncertain whether to laugh or to cry. Actually it was rather touching — but it made her want to kick him. She drew a deep breath. "I hate to be rude —"

"Then don't be. Pretend you don't know me, that I'm just a passenger on the ship, that you're meeting me for the first time."

Betty tried to see him objectively. Tall, loosely muscular, with a blond crew-cut, a face disfigured by a tooth-paste grin, immaculate in faded blue slacks, a yellow T-shirt, a faded blue jacket with dark-blue trim, dark-blue sneakers. "Right out of the band-box," sneered Betty.

"The sea air doesn't improve your disposition. Would you like me to roll in the dirt?"

"I'd like you to jump off the ship." Betty turned back to the Catos.

"I see you've got a friend aboard," said Ora in a bright voice.

"He is nothing of the kind," said Betty flatly. "I had no idea he was coming."

"Awkward," said Alec Cato, "but romantic."

Betty made a disgusted sound. "As romantic as a sucker-fish on a shark."

"You make a very unconvincing shark," said Alec. "An angel-fish perhaps."

"And you, my dear," said Ora, "qualify as a pike, or a skate."

"Oh, we're all queer fish, one way or another."

# 2

The *Garda* swung around the Ferry Building, moving parallel to the Embarcadero. The sun was a murky orange ball low in the sky pouring molten metal through the Golden Gate. The skyline of the city glowed orange, windows gleamed, and a chilly wind blew in from the ocean.

The Latin-American ladies shivered and went below. A dark massive man whom Betty had not seen before came up on deck. He wore a light-gray suit, well-polished yellow shoes, a Panama hat with a very wide brim. His features were blunt, large, rather heavy; he seemed to be smiling. Betty wondered what amused him. He looked casually around the deck, went to stand behind the forward bulkhead. Betty had already examined the two remaining passengers. The elder was a pink-faced man of sixty, plump and agile as a tennis ball. He was bald, with an untidy fringe of gray hair, merry and sly like a debauched kewpie doll. The other was a tall thin lad in well-worn clothes, dark and handsome, but hardly as old as Betty.

Betty counted the passengers: eleven. Three unattached men, not counting the old man with the pink face. Two, omitting Ted. The handsome lad seemed very young. One then: the massive dark man. He turned his head; their glances met. Betty felt a quiver of not unpleasant uneasiness. One man, at least.

The ship passed under the Golden Gate Bridge and out into the Pacific. A bell rang below, signaling dinner.

The mess-hall occupied the forward section of the deck-house. There were three large tables across the forward bulkhead, a single smaller table to the rear. Captain Alberto Frascatore, stocky and gray-haired, with an affable red-nosed face, a mouth glinting with gold teeth, and the mild-appearing Chief Engineer occupied two seats at the central table. They rose when the passengers entered, smiling with the good-fellowship demanded of them in their position as hosts.

There was a period of confusion while the passengers found seats. The four Latin-American ladies settled themselves at the table to the starboard, with a flouncing of skirts and staccato discussion. Alec and Ora Cato made for the table to the port. Betty, ignoring Ted's significant glance, slipped into the seat beside Alec. Ted darted forward, intent on the seat opposite Betty, but a massive shape ambled in front of him. Ted glared, turned and made for a seat at the central table across the aisle from Betty, but this was already occupied by the pink-faced old Bacchus, with the handsome youth beside him.

The only vacant space left was at the small table to the rear of the room. Ted slowly walked to the table, flung himself into one of the chairs, and regarded the room with moody dislike.

Captain Frascatore addressed the Latin-American ladies in Spanish; they tittered appreciatively. Then, in heavily accented English, he spoke to the others. "We must introduce ourselves. I am Captain Frascatore. This is Chief Engineer Buscoglio. These ladies —" he waved his hand "— they are going to El Salvador. They do not speak English, I will not introduce them, but they are very nice all the same. This —" he indicated the big dark man sitting at his right "— is Mr. Mik Finsch. I know him because he has come north with us from El Salvador. He has just sold his *finca*, which is coffee plantation, and now he goes to Europe."

Mik Finsch nodded, his mouth curving up at the corners into what seemed a chronic half-smile. Striking man, thought Betty. Finsch observed her interest; his half-smile trembled into almost a grin. He nodded slightly. Betty quickly turned down her eyes.

"This lady and this gentleman, they are married. I think they are Professor and Mrs. Professor Cato."

"Alec and Ora."

"And this young lady, she is not married. Her name is … ?"

"Betty Haverhill."

"And this gentleman. He is Italian, I think."

"I am Nello di Prieri."

"His father is Marquis di Prieri," said the captain with a glittering gold-toothed grin. "And now we eat. *Zuppa di verdura*. Vegetable soup."

"My name," said Ted loudly, "is Ted Bunpole."

"Yes," said the captain. "I forget. Excuse me. This gentleman is Mr. Bunpole. An odd name, no?"

"We've only been able to trace it to William the Conqueror," said Ted thickly. "It was Bonpoillez then."

"And now it's Bumple." Betty almost said it, but held her tongue.

After the soup came grilled fish with green salad, then roast veal with green beans and potato balls, then fruit, cheese and coffee. On each table were two bottles of wine, white Soave and red Valpolicella.

In spite of the presence of Ted Bunpole at her back, Betty enjoyed herself immensely, chattering with Alec and Ora, and with Mr. Mc-Finch (as Betty had understood the name).

"McFinch?" inquired Harry Mayberry. "That sounds Irish."

"No," said Finsch. "I am not Irish. My father was a Belgian. I never knew my mother. I am a citizen of the Netherlands. My name is Finsch. Mik Finsch."

"He lives in El Salvador," the captain explained once more. "He is a coffee grower."

"No longer," said Finsch. "I have been many things, but now I am nothing." He lifted a bottle of wine, inspected the label. "Valpolicella. A good wine." He turned to Ora. "May I fill your glass?"

"By all means," said Ora.

"And yours?" He held the bottle toward Betty.

"Please," said Betty, staring in fascination at the great hand, almost enveloping the bottle. Black hair grew on the fingers, the nails were clean, and glistened faintly, as if professionally manicured.

Betty flicked her gaze up to Finsch's face, then to the wine, and was careful not to look at Mik Finsch again for several minutes.

Dining among so many citizens of foreign countries, Betty already felt transplanted into a strange land. At first glance they seemed much like the people at home, but there were definite differences: tricks of gesture, unfamiliar mannerisms, odd turns of speech. Still — Betty turned a wry glance to her left — where could she find a more eccentric pair than Alec and Ora? Or to her right, at the next table, a more unctuous pink lizard than Harry Mayberry? Nevertheless, they were no more than departures from a known pattern, houses built of familiar bricks. How could she know the minds of Nello di Prieri, of Mik Finsch, or Captain Frascatore, even of the highly respectable Salvadorean ladies? It was exactly this strangeness, she thought, which made travel interesting.

Captain Frascatore, a garrulous and inquisitive host, made it clear that no one's business would be allowed to remain his own. During dinner and over bitter black Italian coffee, Betty learned:

A: Alec Cato was assistant professor in the English Department at the University of California, on sabbatical leave. He and Ora were considering a visit to Moscow, where they might participate in some kind of international symposium. Possibly they might return to Europe via Kiev, the Crimea and Istanbul.

B: Harry Mayberry owned a dry-cleaning plant in Oakland, across the bay from San Francisco. He had traveled extensively in Mexico, but never before had taken a sea voyage.

C: Nello di Prieri, on the last leg of a rough-and-tumble tour of the world, was an aristocrat by inclination as well as by birth. He professed to embody in himself the purest principles of both pragmatism and idealism. "I try anything! No matter what, if it does not kill me — I try it! Then after, if I like it, I do it again!" He had chewed *ghat* in Iran, betel-nut in Bali, coca in Peru; he had smoked opium in Singapore, marijuana in Los Angeles. Only the Himalaya Mountains had prevented him from riding his Vespa motor-scooter into Nepal.

D: Mik Finsch, sitting back with an air of indulgent boredom, had little to say. His manners were punctilious and formal, with a kind of ponderous grace. When Ora admired a ring he wore on the little finger of his right hand, he said in his measured heavy voice, "Yes, it is nice. It once belonged to a woman of Djakarta. She tried to kill me with a knife—a very terrible knife, hollow and full of poison, like the tooth of a snake. I hit her—here!" He put a great fist across the table against Betty's jaw. "I crushed the bone. The ear-ring fell from her head." He looked placidly at the ring. "It is my souvenir."

"Now he is a coffee planter," said the captain, with an amiable shrug, as if to emphasize the changes which may overtake a man.

Mik Finsch lit a cigar. "Then I was a rubber planter. But I could not stay. They killed many men; they took the women to the mountains for a death more slow, eh? They drove the Dutch away, who had done so much for them. So for four years now I have planted coffee. It is all the same; one must only know how to deal with natives."

E: The Salvadorean ladies had come to Los Angeles to visit relatives, and would disembark at La Libertad, port to the city of San Salvador.

"It is too bad," said the captain, "they did not know we would stop at Los Angeles. So they travel by train to San Francisco. They might have come aboard at Los Angeles."

"How long do we stop in Los Angeles?" asked Betty.

"Not long. Only a few hours. We take some cargo, and one passenger. She will be with you."

"Oh," said Betty. "I wondered if I was to have the cabin all to myself."

"No," said the captain. "But she is very nice. Very beautiful!" He blew a kiss from his fingertips. "She is the wife of our agent at La Libertad; she goes to visit him." He looked around the table. "There will be many beautiful women on the *Garda*. Perhaps we have a beauty contest. You have a bathing suit?" he asked Betty.

"I'll enter a women's beauty contest, if the men put on bathing suits for a men's beauty contest."

The captain showed his gold teeth in great amusement. "Where is the beauty? I am too fat, and my legs are too thin. The crew they will laugh at me."

"I concede right now," said Harry Mayberry. "I'm too bald and I'm white as lard."

"The beauty contest is only for girls," declared Captain Frascatore.

"I'd like to be the judge," said Harry Mayberry. "I've admired beautiful women all my life. Unfortunately from a distance."

Mik Finsch nodded his big dark head. "Beautiful women are excellent things. After all, that is the reason we are on this earth, eh? To drink good wine," he raised his glass, "to have good things to eat, to smoke good cigars, to enjoy the friendship of beautiful women." He drank his wine with satisfaction.

After dinner, Betty, Alec, Ora and Ted went forward to the bow, where they watched the dark water dashing against the cut-water. The sky was overcast, the night pitch-black. Along the shore an occasional spatter of lights could be seen, and once or twice the flicker of headlights along the coast highway. Ted contrived to stand so that his shoulder touched Betty's. She moved irritably away.

Ted turned his head down to her. Betty could not read his expression, but she knew it was angry and sullen. Too bad. Ted would simply have to suffer. If he thought that dogging her footsteps would soften her, he was wrong.

Ora Cato said, "I'm getting cold. I think I'll go back. I want to straighten out the cabin."

"I think I'll do the same," said Betty.

Ted took Betty's arm. "I want to talk to you."

Betty pulled away. "I'm going back where it's warm." She followed quickly on the heels of Alec and Ora. Ted remained behind staring bitterly toward the shore.

On the way to the deck-house Betty thrust aside every trace of pity; she could accept absolutely no responsibility for Ted. Of course — and Betty's conscience gave an uneasy twinge — there had been times when for lack of anything better to do, she had flirted with Ted, teasing him, blowing hot and cold. Cruel perhaps — but not consciously cruel. Betty had only been testing her weapons: a kitten sharpening its claws on a handy piece of furniture…Well, that was all in the past. No more flirting — certainly not with Ted. With Mik Finsch, perhaps. A small mild flirtation. Of course she must be careful, because Mik Finsch was clearly no Ted Bunpole, to be put in his place with a sharp word. Mik Finsch was a man of the world; he would be over-powering; her ego would count for nothing.

She passed from the darkness of the deck into the brightness of the deck-house, climbed two flights of steel stairs, sauntered down the corridor toward her cabin. The ship was still unfamiliar; she took the wrong turning and almost blundered into the wheel-house. She retraced her steps, listening to the sounds of the ship. From somewhere, apparently the radio room, came a *beep-beep beep-beep-beep*, rising in pitch, cutting off abruptly. Alone in the dim corridor, lined with blank oak doors, Betty suddenly became nervous and was glad to reach the security of Cabin #2.

She unpacked and arranged her belongings, considering her fellow passengers. And Ted. Poor silly irritating Ted.

*Rap-rap.* A cautious diffident knock.

"Who is it?" called Betty.

"Me. Ted."

"What do you want?"

"I want to talk to you."

She ran to the door, flung it open, prepared to deliver a tongue-lashing. Ted stood in the doorway, looking forlorn and dejected. "Oh come on in," said Betty. "But you can't stay long because I'm going to bed."

Ted came in, sat down on one of the beds. He looked around the room. "My cabin is smaller than this. In fact I'm in the hospital."

"The hospital? Why?"

"I guess there was nothing left."

"I thought you were in with Mr. Finsch."

Ted scowled. "He has a cabin to himself. Which suits me very well." He looked at the shelf over Betty's bed. "What did you bring to read?"

"Highbrow stuff. Nothing you'd be interested in."

"Quite the wit, aren't you? Someday I'm going to blister your fanny."

"Is that all you've got to say? You were so all-fired anxious to get in. Now you're here. Talk."

Ted stared, ran his hand through his blond crew-cut. "All right, I will. I want to tell you why I came along."

"I know why. To dog my footsteps."

"That's about it. I'm planning to marry you —"

"Don't start that again!"

"— and until I do, I'm taking care of you."

"Ted," said Betty patiently. "I don't want you taking care of me!"

"Whether you like it or not, you've got it. You *need* it! You're such an innocent, such a lamb for the slaughter!"

For ten seconds Betty was at a loss for words. She took a deep breath. "I am not going to marry you. Never. Get that through your skull. I do not love you. I do not hate you. I just don't care. One thing I must emphasize: if you think you're going to follow me all over Europe, supervising my every move, you're wrong. Because I won't have it."

Ted became furious. "You're a conceited little witch!"

"If you've said all you came to say, you can leave."

Ted jumped to his feet. "No, it's not all. I wanted to warn you. To be careful."

"Careful? Of what?" asked Betty, although she knew very well.

"Of Finsch. I've seen that kind before. He'll eat a little girl like you right up."

"Mr. Bumple," said Betty in a clear voice, "don't you give me credit for any intelligence? Or character? Or common sense? — not to mention minding your own business?"

"I saw you," said Ted thickly. "Throwing sheep's-eyes, and him smirking like a bear up to his neck in honey."

"Mr. Bumple —"

"And stop calling me Bumple. My name is Bunpole."

"— I don't recall inviting you on this trip. I don't know how to say it politely — but will you please not annoy me? Will you please get off the ship at Los Angeles?"

"No. I won't."

"Then I had better remind you that I am almost twenty-two years old. I'll throw sheep's-eyes at Finsch, and anything else if I feel in the mood."

Ted opened the door. "I warn you, there'll be trouble. I warn you!"

"Goodnight Ted."

The door slammed. Betty sat down on the bed, twisting her fingers together. That damn Ted! He was as much of a nuisance as Mother. The idea started a new, rather startling and vastly irritating chain of thought. Betty sat thinking. It was possible, quite possible. Tomorrow she'd verify her idea, and if things were as she suspected... Betty blew out her cheeks. There would be fireworks.

The cabin was warm, with heat seeping through the steel decks from the engine-room. Betty opened the porthole to its fullest extent, locked the door, undressed and went to bed.

She lay awake in the dark. Through the porthole came the hiss of moving water. She thought she heard voices somewhere, subdued and unintelligible... She wondered what her new room-mate would be like. The wife of a shipping agent at La Libertad. Beautiful, according to the captain...

When she awoke, gray light was entering the porthole. She looked at her watch. Seven o'clock. Betty swung sleepily out of bed, washed her face, scrubbed her teeth, brushed her hair, dressed in blue jeans, a white polo shirt, sandals, and went below.

After breakfast she took one of her books to a protected corner of the deck, and settled down, relaxed and happy, reading and watching the mountainous gray-green coast. In spite of Ted the world seemed a pleasant place. Nello came up on deck, looked in her direction. Betty instantly became absorbed in her book. Nello turned away.

Harry Mayberry appeared, croaking a sea-chanty, and persuaded Nello to try a game of quoits. It looked like fun and Betty was on the verge of asking if she could play too, when Mik Finsch appeared. He stood looking around the horizon, puffing luxurious clouds of smoke from a new cigar, then drew a chair up beside Betty. He stretched out his legs. "Ah! It is good to rest. There will be much time to rest on the *Garda*."

Betty agreed.

"I have not always traveled so quietly," said Finsch. "During the war I owned a schooner." He shook his head, his half-smile rueful. "There were whites who fled the Japanese; there were Japanese who fled the whites. It was a very dangerous business. But very much money." He puffed at his cigar.

"You worked for the Japanese?" asked Betty in astonishment.

"Why not? Their money was good. I carried them where they wished to go."

"But didn't the government disapprove?"

"Of course. But what of that? They could prove nothing. There were many strange affairs in those times."

"You seem to have led an eventful life," said Betty with quiet sarcasm.

Finsch made a gesture of whimsical deprecation. "I have seen many things. I have done many things. Men have tried to kill me. They have not succeeded."

"You killed them first?"

"Is not that a law of nature?"

Betty turned, settled into her chair, picked up her book. Finsch looked at her in amusement. "You are shocked? You disapprove?"

Betty said after a moment of reflection, "Why, yes. I suppose so."

Finsch's smile became broad, revealing great white teeth. He drew at his cigar with great enjoyment. "You say yes — but you mean no. Women are peculiar, but everywhere the same."

Betty started to make an indignant protest, but Finsch's voice continued evenly. "At the prize-fight they call the loudest. At the bull-fight they faint with joy when the red blood flows."

"In my opinion," said Betty, "only perverts go to bull-fights."

Finsch shrugged amiably. "No matter. You need not disapprove. My life is now quiet. This is better. To sit beside a lovely young lady, to smoke a cigar, to talk of wise things — it is the best part of life."

"I hope those are expensive cigars," said Betty thoughtfully.

"Eh?" inquired Finsch.

"I wouldn't like to be classed with a poor cigar in your calendar of enjoyments."

Finsch looked at the cigar critically, shook his big dark head in reproach. "Now you make sport of me. You think I care more for my cigars than other things. Am I so very ancient?"

"I don't know. Am I so very young?"

Finsch laughed. "You ask a dangerous question. One should never discuss age with a woman. Only experience. I am experienced. Experience is not age. I am no longer foolish." Finsch glanced briefly at Nello di Prieri. "I am old enough to know the good things of life and I know how to enjoy them… Ah, here is your fiancé."

"My what?"

Ted Bunpole came up on the deck, glanced quickly back and forth, scowled when he saw Betty and Finsch sitting together. He went to the rail, inspected the passing water. Then, without looking toward Betty, he sidled absent-mindedly along the rail, and seemed to be surprised when he found himself standing beside her.

"Ted," said Betty thoughtfully, "I wonder how Mr. Finsch came to the conclusion that you were my fiancé."

Ted stared defiantly down at her. "I told him."

"You shouldn't lie to Mr. Finsch, Ted. He doesn't lie to you."

"That's how it is for all practical purposes."

Betty felt a great fatigue. It was hard to be patient. "No, Ted. How many times must I tell you?"

Alec and Ora Cato came up.

"What's new? Anything exciting?"

"Yes, in a way," said Ted with a ghastly grin. "I'm trying to convince Betty that we're getting married."

Betty's patience approached the brink. "You're trying to brainwash me. I'll make a public announcement. I am not marrying Ted Bumple. I don't care a fig for Ted Bumple. I wish Ted Bumple would take the veil, or fly to the moon, or drown."

"That seems fairly definite," said Alec.

Finsch placidly smoked his cigar; Ora peered at Ted as if he were a two-headed calf. Ted stood rigid and white, the ghastly grin smeared across his face. There was no graceful retreat; he sought to save face by means of facetious obduracy. "What Betty says doesn't count. She's crazy about me, but won't admit it. It's all settled — we're getting married. And I won't have any interference."

Betty's patience flickered out. "I wouldn't touch you if you were the last man alive! You're a pest! I came on this trip to get rid of you, and you follow me aboard! Don't talk to me again! I'll hit you with a belaying pin, if I can find one!"

She jumped to her feet, ran down to her cabin, where she flung herself on the bed and lay staring at the ceiling with flinty eyes. That damn Ted! All sympathy for him was gone. And to think that this was only the first day at sea!

After a while she found a book and managed to read. At lunchtime she had simmered down and felt faintly embarrassed about the scene on the top deck. Well, there was nothing to do but put a good face on it.

# 3

For lunch there was a first course of *antipasto*, then *spaghetti al burro*, then *calamari alla romana* with *ensalata mista*, then *fegato alla veneziana con fagiolini*, then *frutta* and *caffè*. The *antipasto* was ham, pickles, olives, sardines; *spaghetti al burro* was ordinary spaghetti drenched with butter and parmesan cheese; *calamari* were small crisp bits of fried octopus, served with a mixed salad; *fegato alla veneziana con fagiolini* was liver and onions with string beans; the *frutta* was an orange; *caffè* the usual dark black Italian decoction. Betty tried to be gay but Alec and Ora had little to say, and Mik Finsch seemed content to regard her quizzically, under half-closed eyelids. Ted left the mess-hall quickly, and Betty saw him through the porthole wandering disconsolately up to the bow.

After lunch there was nothing much to do: in fact, thought Betty, there would be little to do at any time, except sleep, eat, read, play cards, talk. She climbed to the top deck and found Mik Finsch lounging in a deck-chair. Two other activities suggested themselves: flirting with Mik Finsch and avoiding Ted Bunpole. She settled herself into the chair beside Finsch. He turned his head and looked her over with candid intentness.

Well, why not? Curled up in the deck-chair, she knew she looked attractive: the blue jeans tight over her legs, the polo shirt certainly not loose. Mik Finsch made no secret of his interest. It seemed as if his animal magnetism, or whatever it was called, was much stronger than usual. Betty felt relaxed, but not at all drowsy — in fact, rather vividly alive. Almost excited.

"This overcast is usual of the sea along here," said Finsch. "We will have it for two days more."

"Oh?" Interesting. Finsch was an interesting man. He leaned toward her, and Betty's skin prickled. "Your fiancé — will he object to my talking to you?"

Betty laughed. "You know what I care for his objections."

"A difficult situation."

"For Ted. Not for me. Do you know, I think my mother talked him into coming along, to keep an eye on me. I wouldn't be surprised if she bought his ticket. He doesn't have any money."

"Hm," said Finsch. "Do you require such close watching?"

"I guess I do," said Betty. "I'm getting it." She felt vaguely alarmed. The conversation was getting out of hand. A smoky warmth had entered Finsch's voice, there was a self-conscious contralto sound to her own. "Why did you sell your coffee plantation?"

Finsch considered judiciously. "I sold for three reasons. First, I was offered an excellent price — more than a hundred thousand dollars — by the Atlantic and Pacific Company. Secondly, politics and personal friendship controls everything in Central America. If you bribe well, if you are a relative, if you are able to blackmail — then you prosper. If not, it is very hard. Third, and most important, I have become bored with Central America. So I sold. I came north to San Francisco to sign the papers and receive my money; I go now to El Salvador for my few belongings. I go ashore, I come back on the *Garda* — it is simple as that."

Ted Bunpole came up on deck, glowered toward Betty and Finsch, lowered himself into a deck-chair, seemed to go to sleep. Presently he rose to his feet, stood swaying with a peculiar set look on his face. He turned and half-walked, half-ran to the stairs.

"He is sea-sick," said Mik Finsch, grinning widely.

"Sea-sick?" Betty had fortified herself with Bonamine. "Poor Ted... Well, I suppose it serves him right."

Finsch rose to his feet. "Come with me; I will show you something."

Betty hesitated, various levels of her mind churning all together. "This is it!" said one voice breathlessly. "Careful," said another, "he's very clever and very attractive." "But you are clever and attractive too," was a third, rather idiotic opinion. "You'll get in trouble," warned a fourth voice. "What the hell," said a fifth. "You're able to look out for yourself. You've told everybody so a dozen times." "Ted will be furious," said a sixth voice.

Finsch was holding out his hand. Ignoring all the voices Betty took hold and jumped lightly to her feet. She noticed Finsch turn a quick look to left and right as they left the deck, almost furtively, as if he thought it best not to be seen by anyone. Betty, blushing, looked right and left too. She felt the same way.

Finsch ushered her along the passageway, swept open the oak door of his cabin with the grandeur of a baron.

Betty paused, looked back at him over her shoulder. "I shouldn't be doing this," she said in a subdued voice.

Finsch took her elbows, eased her forward, closed the door. The cabin contained a leather-covered settee, a desk, a chest of drawers and a bed. Finsch had arranged his possessions with spartan neatness: an ivory brush and comb, a bottle of cologne, an electric razor. Under the bunk a large leather suitcase was precisely located.

Betty stood gingerly in the center of the room. She felt stiff and awkward. "Sit down," said Finsch, waving to the settee. He opened the closet, brought out a bottle.

"I don't care for anything," said Betty quickly. Up on the top deck there had been a different atmosphere to the whole matter. The cabin seemed confining; Finsch looked large and no longer magnetic; the bed was embarrassingly in evidence, it seemed to be everywhere she looked.

Finsch continued his preparations, smiling his half-humorous smile. "I will pour you just a taste. It is the right time for a glass of good brandy. Just a trifle — so. And then —" he drew forth his suitcase, set it on the bed, opened it. Among the clothes lay a large automatic pistol, black, with ivory insets along the butt.

"Heavens!" exclaimed Betty. "Why the arsenal?"

Finsch picked up the gun, hefted it affectionately. "It is my oldest friend." He removed the magazine, offered the gun to Betty. "For several years I worked with the Javanese secret police. I had many enemies. I kept my eyes wide, I will tell you."

Betty gave the gun back to Finsch. "And your enemies pursue you everywhere?"

"No. No longer. This was long ago, before *merdeka*. Now I am just as you see me, an idle man. But I learned that one must always be able to protect oneself. For instance, see here." He handed Betty a black plastic capsule. "Do you know what this is?"

"No."

"It is gas. And these?"

"Those are brass knuckles."

"Yes. And this is a little *kris*, like a snake. Of course I do not keep these things for use. They are my souvenirs. But here. This is something I wish to show you." Finsch picked up a green object, looked at it carefully, handed it to Betty: a small sphere of jade, incised with three parallel bands of Chinese characters. "What do you think of it?"

"It's very beautiful, naturally…What is it?"

"It is a —" Finsch rubbed his chin. "I do not know the English word. A sign, a piece of magic."

"Talisman?"

"Talisman. That is a good word. This is my talisman. It is very old. These characters make a poem. They read:

> *The stars are fragments of a demon sun, who*
> *sought to ravish the moon and was destroyed.*
> *He wept green tears of pain, ninety-nine green*
> *tears, of which this orb is the seventeenth.*

Betty cupped the sphere between her palms. It felt cool and suave. "How old is it?"

"I do not know," said Finsch. "Some say five thousand years. Some say no more than three thousand. It was a treasure of the old court at Peking. The man from whom I had it was the Imperial torturer." Finsch shook his head. "He was a strange man, a poet, with a very strange philosophy."

Betty abruptly gave the ball back to Finsch.

"You are distressed?" asked Finsch with concern. "That is wrong. One must take the world as it is, as many people of the world find it: a purgatory, where only the very strong or the very lucky find peace."

"But the world isn't like that! A person can be as happy as they want to be!"

Finsch raised his eyebrows. "It is wrong to think of happiness, or of good, or evil. They do not exist. They are for the priests. There are many pleasant things in the world, but to enjoy them, we must reach out for them. Is that happiness? Perhaps. So we are in agreement after all."

Betty laughed uncertainly. "I'm not so sure. We say the same words, but we mean different things."

Finsch shrugged amiably. He turned the jade ball over in his fingers, put it carefully into his suitcase, then brought forth a small flask in a vermilion lacquer case. "This is what I set out to find. I am absentminded." He drew the bottle from the case. The label was exquisitely printed with hundreds of flowers in pale pure colors. Finsch carefully poured five or six drops from the flask into each glass of brandy.

"What is that?" asked Betty in mingled curiosity and suspicion. There were no conflicting voices in her mind now.

"It is an essence from Java. It is called 'Flowers of Love'. Taste it, it is good."

Betty lifted her glass, smelled of the contents. Aphrodisiac? Dope? Knockout drops? The brandy exhaled a faint perfume, more tart than sweet, closer to lime than musk. She tasted; it seemed ordinary brandy. The 'Flowers of Love' was only barely perceptible. She tasted a second time. Just brandy. Betty put the glass down, rose briskly to her feet. "I think I'll —"

Mik Finsch rose from the chair. His great body seemed to fill the room. Betty swayed back.

"You must taste once more," said Finsch. "That is the — what do you say? — the ritual." He handed her the glass, his smile negligent and good-humored.

Betty forbore to ask the meaning of the ritual. She took the glass, wet her lips, set the glass on the chest of drawers. "Now I —" Mik Finsch put his great hands on her shoulders, pulled her forward and upward. Smiling his easy half-smile, he kissed her. His chin rasped her face, he smelled strongly of his cigars.

Betty swayed back, wiped her mouth with the back of her hand.

Mik Finsch, holding her about the waist, smiled whimsically down at her. "You like me, eh? I like you."

Betty stared at him, paralyzed into speechlessness. There were no voices in her mind at all, conflicting or otherwise, only inarticulate apprehension and weakness. She pushed at Finsch's arms; they were like bars of steel. He bent his head, kissed her again, her mouth, her forehead, her neck. "No," she gasped. "No! Please don't!"

He led her to the bed, seated himself, drew her across his lap.

"No!" exclaimed Betty fiercely. "That's enough! Dammit. Let go of me!"

Finsch was grinning, paying no attention to her protests. One arm encircled her shoulders, the other tugged at the zipper to the side of her jeans. This is ridiculous, thought Betty. I hardly know the man, and he's taking the most extreme liberties. She tried to make her voice sound firm and definite. "Please, Mr. Finsch, I have absolutely no —" He kissed her; the words strangled in her throat. She began to feel panicky. He was strong as a bear. She could scream. Would anyone hear? She'd look a fool. The zipper slid down, the jeans gave loosely at her waist. This was dreadful. She had brought it on herself, now she must face the consequences. She felt limp and weak, she felt ashamed, she felt angry. "Will you *stop*! I'm leaving, right now!"

The door opened, and there was Ted. Such was the state of her mind that Betty felt no surprise. She might have predicted it. The whole situation was farcical.

"Well, Ted," said Betty, "as you see, you are disturbing us."

Ted seemed a maniac. He bellowed something, sprang forward. Finsch rolled back, tilting Betty, loose jeans and all, across his chest. He raised his knees, striking Betty a tooth-rattling thump which impeded him and saved Ted a kick in the stomach.

Ted jumped at Finsch's throat, with Betty still between them. The three rolled on the bed. Betty scrambled free, and holding up her jeans, ducked frantically into the corner of the room.

Ted's mouth hung loose, his eyes were glassy. Finsch seemed calm, even contemptuous. Ted rushed forward; Finsch's knee jerked up, but Ted stopped short, swung a terrible blow into Finsch's face, directly under the cheek-bone.

Finsch's massive head quivered, a red bloom appeared on his cheek. His grin widened, his teeth showed. He put his hands down to the bed, tried to rise; Ted struck again, and Betty winced at the sound of the blow. Finsch bled from the corner of his mouth. He was too heavy to give under the blow, too thick-skulled to be knocked cold; he could only bruise and bleed.

Ted was laughing now, savage and vindictive. The fight was releasing all his pent emotion. Finsch, grinning stupidly, again tried to rise from the bed, and this time he gained his feet; he stood solid as a tree. "Ah!" croaked Finsch in satisfaction. He swung a great windmilling blow at Ted, which would have exploded Ted through the door into the hall, but Ted stepped close, plunged his fist into Finsch's belly, and when Finsch's knee rose, he grabbed the crook of the knee, lifted, hurled Finsch backward over the bed, so that Finsch's head rang on the bulkhead.

Betty came to her senses. She was screaming; she had been screaming for some time. The room was suddenly boiling with excited men in sun-tan uniforms: the captain, the ship's officers.

Ted let out a deep breath, dropped his arms, irritably pushed away the Italians who were tugging at him, imploring him to peace. Betty looked at him in surprise: a new Ted; a dynamic, efficient, alarming Ted.

"Get this straight, Finsch," said Ted, panting. "Don't pull any more of your stunts, not on this ship, or you'll get a worse beating than you got now." He looked at Betty. "And you. I've been watching for something like this."

Poor Ted. He needed only to open his mouth, and from admirable Ted, he became foolish, pompous, annoying Ted.

Ted went on to complete the job, and to extinguish the last vestige of amiability in Betty. "From now on," he declared, "you're my girl. I'm marrying you as soon as we get off this ship. If you even look sideways at this bumpkin, I'll thrash both of you."

Betty almost wept with rage. "Why don't you mind your own damn business?" Not an original remark, but fervor supplied the sting of a new-coined phrase.

Finsch said gently, "Come. That was no fight. It was a coward's blow. Let us go out on the deck. I will show this lad what it means to fight."

"No, no," cried the captain in a sharp voice. "No more of this foolishness!"

"I cannot allow it," said Finsch. "He crows like a dunghill rooster."

"Mr. Finsch!" said the captain. "No more of this; it is not right for the passengers to fight. Not on my ship. It is not to be done! You must shake hands."

Finsch said nothing, but turning his back, went to the basin, wet a towel, pressed it to his face.

Ted, with an infallible instinct for the inept, said, "Come along, Betty. You're going with me."

"I am doing no such thing! I came here of my own accord; I'll leave when I'm good and ready. For the last time, will you leave me alone?" She turned desperately to the captain. "Can't you stop him from hounding me? Can't you put him off the ship?"

"No, no, I cannot do that." The captain shook his head in irritation. "I must ask you all to act like ladies and gentlemen. You put me in a difficult position."

Ted stepped forward, tapped the captain's chest with one finger, pointed with the other hand at Finsch. "Are you going to let the little fool be taken in by that swine of a Dutchman? I ask you. Are you going to stand for it?"

The captain broke out into a sweat of embarrassment and annoyance. "It is not my business," he barked. "I cannot teach passengers how to act. Only my crew. But I think that you intruded into this cabin. It is not your cabin. If Mr. Finsch wishes to offer Miss Haverhill a glass of cognac—" the captain held out his hands, shrugged "—then it is not your business, it is not mine. Those are the rules of the company."

Ted slowly turned toward the door. Finsch said to his back, "I will show you what it means to fight."

"Any time," Ted said in a dull voice. "Any time at all."

"No!" exclaimed the captain, his eyebrows bristling. "There must be no more disturbance. That is also a company rule. It is not safe. I warn you both," he shook his finger first at Finsch, then at Ted, "no more of this matter. After all, you are here for pleasure. Why not be reasonable?"

Ted, pushing through the ship's officers, left the room. Finsch stood by the basin. "He surprised me," he told Betty. "He knows nothing. He will regret this."

The captain shook his head in disapproval and departed, taking his underlings with him.

Betty looked sardonically at Finsch. "Well, that was nice. You and your 'Flowers of Love'."

Finsch patted the towel against his bruised cheek, his lips pulled back into a grimace of seeming joviality. "I will teach your college boy a lesson. He will not bother us again."

"There won't be an 'again', and I wouldn't annoy Ted, if I were you. He's a bone-head, but he's good at games. Like football and boxing."

"Ha!" said Finsch in savage amusement. "You think I am a baby? If you speak my name along the Sunda Coast, in Djakarta, in Palembang, you will understand."

"I understand enough. I understand I was a fool for coming in here. I understand that everyone will be looking at me sidewise for the rest of the trip. It's my own fault. I'm not blaming you. You look just as much a fool as I do."

Finsch, who had been bending over the basin with his towel, turned his great dark head. "That is not a good thing to say."

"Perhaps not, but I don't care. I'll go now. Thanks for the brandy." She swung the door open, marched out into the passage.

She went to her room. Ted Bunpole was sitting on her bed. "No no no!" cried Betty in desperation.

"I want to talk to you."

"Get out of here! You're driving me crazy! I can't stand the sight of you!"

Ted rose to his feet, his face pasty. "Do you mean that?"

"How many times do I have to tell you? Can't you take a hint?"

Ted nodded slowly, in dreary amusement. "The Dutchman gets into your pants. You won't even hold my hand…Yes. I can take a hint." He went slowly to the door, opened it, stood fumbling with the knob.

"Please, Ted — don't harass me any more."

"I told your mother I'd look after you," said Ted dully. "But that's over. You can go to hell any way you like."

Betty said nothing. She turned away, her cheeks burning. The door closed. Click, went the latch. Slow and soft and final.

Betty flung herself down on the bed, buried her face in her arms, and lay sobbing.

# 4

The bell sounded for dinner. Betty sat up slowly, feeling red-eyed, cross and languid. The least of her inclinations was to go down to the mess-hall. But she had to go. Keeping to her room would only make things worse. Best to brazen it out. She changed into a simple blue dress, washed her face, examined herself critically, went below.

The Salvadorean ladies were already eating their soup. Harry Mayberry, Nello and the captain, talking brightly, fell silent when Betty appeared, then continued in a slightly different key. Mik Finsch nodded politely as Betty seated herself. Talcum camouflaged but failed to conceal his bruises. Alec and Ora Cato inspected Betty with frank interest. Ted was nowhere to be seen, nor did he appear during the meal. Finsch had little to say. What a strange situation, thought Betty: dining across the table from a man who only a few hours before had attempted, if not rape, at least a very earnest seduction!

Finsch ate with methodical relish, completely nonchalant. Betty watched him surreptitiously. Each of his movements conveyed a sense of inexorable force. The strokes of his knife through meat were Destiny itself, that neither meat, gristle nor bone could resist. She studied the heavy face with the detachment of an anatomist: the slabs of cheek muscle, the massive bones, the big blunt features, the coarse black hair. Peculiar, the humorous and tolerant twist to the mouth! Did he always feel so calm and amused?

She left the table with Alec and Ora. They were bound for the top deck, and Betty followed them up the stairs. At the door to Cabin #2 she paused indecisively. It was too early to go to bed, but still…

Ora made the decision for her. "Come on up with us. The fresh air will do you good. And we're dying with curiosity."

Why not? thought Betty. She wanted to talk, and certainly it was better to satisfy their curiosity than to have them indulging in lurid speculation. "I'll get a sweater."

They drew chairs around to face west across the Pacific. The overcast glowed under a half-moon like frosted glass, and the water gave off the gray sheen of slate.

"Tell us everything," said Ora. "We've heard only the wildest rumors."

"Well —"

Alec had brought out his pipe and was filling it. "If I may say so, this curiosity Ora refers to is hers alone. She's got a scurrilous imagination. She should have been a sociologist. Don't talk if you don't care to."

"No, not at all. I —"

"Good, kind Alec!" said Ora. "Charitable, Christ-like Alec, who always takes two bites to eat a marshmallow."

"Ha, ha, my dear woman," said Alec indulgently. "It's all one to me. I merely lack any taste for scurrility."

"What a word! It's natural to be interested in other people!"

"I agree. Natural and healthy."

Betty cleared her throat. "After all —"

"Scurrility is good therapy," Alec continued. "It soothes our own guilt feelings."

"Speak for yourself!"

"If we feel no guilt, we can enjoy other people's vices without incurring the penalties. Hence the popularity of scandal-mongering."

Ora sighed in disgust. "Pay no attention to him. Sometimes he sinks out of sight."

"Very well," said Alec, lighting his pipe. "I'll be quiet. Tell us what happened."

Betty now had no idea where to begin. She said tentatively, "It's just one of those situations…In a year I suppose I'll laugh about it…"

Alec and Ora uttered sympathetic phrases, which Betty hardly heard; she was lost in the events of the afternoon. "What puzzles me, how did I get involved in such a mess? I went down to Finsch's cabin for a drink. Nothing wrong with that, I keep telling myself. I suppose — to be honest — I'd been flirting. He took me seriously." She took a deep breath. "Anyway — it was like a car wreck. Things happened fast. Woof! For once I was glad to see Ted. He gave Finsch a terrible thrashing."

"Ah! That explains friend Finsch's bruise," said Alec.

Betty laughed mournfully. "Basically that's the situation. I feel cheap. Finsch has a bruise. Ted is off grieving. None of us came out very well."

Alec waved his pipe. "I wouldn't take it too seriously, especially you and Ted. You're just a couple of kids. For Finsch it's different. He has a good opinion of himself, and he's lost face."

"Yes," said Betty in a subdued voice. "He threatened Ted—told him he'd show him what fighting really meant."

"Finsch seems to be a poor loser," Alec murmured thoughtfully. "If I were Ted…" His voice trailed off.

"I must say I feel sorry for Ted," said Ora indignantly. "He's only trying to do the gallant thing!"

Betty sighed. "He's an ass. But I feel sorry for him too. I wish I could press a button and whisk Ted back to San Francisco. Oh how he gets on my nerves! He moons around me. I feel like Ben Bolt. I don't want to be responsible for Ted's happiness; it's wrong to have such power over somebody else! I don't want it!"

"It seems as if you've got it," said Alec. He rose to his feet. "Let's see if we can scare up a fourth for bridge."

"I'm going to talk to Ted," said Betty decidedly. "Maybe I can persuade him to leave the ship at Los Angeles."

Ora patted Betty's arm. "Just don't get into any more situations."

"I won't."

# 5

Betty found Ted's cabin after five minutes of wandering along the corridors. She knocked on the oak panel. There was no answer. She knocked again, opened the door a trifle. "Ted? Are you there?"

The room was quiet. Betty opened the door wider, turned on the light. The room was empty. The pillow showed a dent, the spread was wrinkled. Ted's suitcase, open but not unpacked, occupied the chair.

Betty switched off the light, closed the door.

She descended to the main deck, walked forward to the bow, where she expected to find Ted leaning on the rail, enjoying his misery.

No Ted. Where was the idiot? She returned to the deck-house, looked into the mess-hall, to find Alec, Ora, Nello and Harry Mayberry playing cards. No Ted.

She climbed to the boat deck, mounted a ladder to the bridge, looked into the wheel-house. The binnacle glowed, revealing the quartermaster's face, intent on the quivering dial of the compass. The mate on watch stood looking through the porthole. Betty climbed another ladder to the top deck; sure enough, someone stood out on the wing of the flying bridge.

Betty approached. The man turned his head: it was Mik Finsch. Betty could smell his cigar and see the glow of its tip.

"Good evening," said Finsch, his voice placid and untroubled.

"I was looking for Ted," said Betty.

"I have not seen him," said Finsch. "Perhaps he is up at the bow, or in his cabin. Would you like me to look?"

"No thanks. I'll probably find him in the mess-hall."

"Ah, but you must not go so soon. See how the moon lights the clouds!"

Betty tried to extricate herself without betraying her nervousness. "I rather wanted to find Ted."

"He does not matter, for now we talk. The night is beautiful, is it not?"

"Yes, very beautiful. But now —"

"And now what do you think?"

Betty, already turning away, stopped short. If Finsch showed no shame, why should she? "Think?" she asked coldly. "About what?"

"It was not so bad, eh? I am not such a bad man after all."

"If you're referring to this afternoon, I'd rather forget it."

"Very well; we shall forget it." He flourished his hand; the tip of his cigar made a dull red streak in the dark. "It is forgotten, and we start once again."

"We do nothing of the sort."

"But if you have forgotten —"

"I still retain a certain vague recollection."

"Excellent! For your age, you are very wise. You see reality for what it is, and you are not angry."

Betty laughed hollowly. "I'm trying — with difficulty — to remain impersonal."

Finsch shook his head ruefully. "Someday you will think back, and perhaps you will say, 'Poor Mik Finsch, I was unjust.'"

"Anything is possible, Mr. Finsch." He was obstinate, thought Betty, with a hide thick as an elephant's. But she was no less obstinate, as

Ted could testify. Where was Ted anyway? She went to the bulwark, searched the forward deck. Under the gunmetal overcast, shapes merged together; there was nothing to be seen but the bulk of the ship and the foam glimmering away from the sides.

Finsch's voice came from close over her shoulder. "It is a long trip to Genoa. I do not know Genoa well. Paris is far better. Perhaps we might meet in Paris. What a coincidence, eh? There are many amusing things to do in Paris, many excellent restaurants…"

Betty moved away from the rail, ducking past Finsch. "I don't think we'll meet in Paris."

"We will see," said Finsch with vast good humor. "Women are much alike. The louder they cry no! the more they mean yes."

"I'm different. The louder I cry no, the more I mean no."

Finsch chuckled indulgently. "I see that I have annoyed you. But still you wonder about me. What is he up to? I will be frank. I think men and women were put here on this world for each other's benefit. It is like the air. Why is it here? It is free, for us to breathe. The trees bear fruit. Why? For men to eat. That is natural, eh? And it is natural—"

"But I am not air; air is free, and I'm not. I am not a tree, I do not bear fruit. I am a human being, with ideas of my own about air and trees. I definitely am not here for your benefit!"

Throwing his head up, Finsch laughed. "There! You have said it! You feel better! And now—we will be friends. What do you say?"

"In another minute," said Betty, "you'll be asking me to your cabin for a glass of brandy."

"Why not? We will drink and we will be friends again."

Betty's restraint began to wear thin. "Friends! You tried to attack me this afternoon. You haven't shown the slightest sign of regret!"

Finsch waved his cigar. "I am a man! Must I regret losing my head over a pretty girl?"

Betty laughed curtly. "Well, I've decided not to have you arrested for assault, if that's any comfort. You've been punished enough."

" 'Punished'?" Finsch seemed as lazy and complacent as before, but there was a new note in his voice. "You think I have been punished? Is that what you think?"

"I'm going below," said Betty.

"One moment." Finsch threw his cigar over the rail. "I had hoped to forget this afternoon. That monkey is not worth considering. He is hysterical, like a woman. But now I see I must set things right. The puppy must have the whipping it deserves. No one will say that the young college boy has punished me. I will show differently."

From the deep shade beside the funnel came the scrape of a chair. Ted lurched out into the open. "I heard you. I heard the whole thing!"

"Ted!" cried Betty mortified. "You've been eavesdropping!"

"What of it? So the Dutchman wants more, does he? I'm the boy who'll give it to him."

"Ted, have you gone crazy?"

"Shut up. Come on, blow-hard; haul your fat ass down on the hatch, in the light." He crossed the deck, descended the stairs.

"Mr. Finsch!" cried Betty. "Don't pay any attention to him." But Finsch had thrust her aside, and was striding after Ted.

Betty hesitated, then ran down the forward ladder to the bridge. The mate on watch looked around in surprise. "Is the captain here?" cried Betty. Not waiting for an answer, she ran through the wheel-house, to the captain's cabin. She knocked on the door, flung it open, but the cabin was empty. She hurried down to the main deck, along the corridor to the mess-hall. She rushed in, looked feverishly around. Alec, Ora, Harry Mayberry and Nello sat playing rummy; the captain and the chief engineer leaned over a chess board. Betty ran forward. "Captain, you've got to stop it; they'll hurt each other."

"What's this?" The captain looked up, eyes narrow.

"It's Ted and Mr. Finsch, they're fighting."

The captain jumped to his feet. "Where is this?"

"Out on the deck."

The captain marched from the room, with Betty at his elbow — down the corridor and out on the after deck, where a deck-light shone brightly on the No. 2 hatch.

In the center of the hatch Ted and Mik Finsch had squared off. Finsch appeared composed and indolent; Ted looked red-faced and wild-eyed.

"Stop this at once!" bellowed the captain, but neither Ted nor Finsch paid him heed. Ted jabbed with his left, teasing Finsch; Finsch jumped forward, swung his right arm like a club. Ted ducked away, jabbed again and bloodied Finsch's nose.

The captain marched between, thrust them apart. "No more of this! The next man to strike a blow, I put him off the ship!"

"He keeps asking for it," said Ted, a glassy-eyed grin on his face. "If he behaves himself he won't get hurt."

Finsch applied a handkerchief to his nose. "Perhaps it might be better, Captain, to allow me to whip this puppy..."

Ted chuckled and turning, jumped off the hatch. Finsch stared after him.

"There must be no more," said the captain. "If you hurt yourself, then you sue the company, and they say, 'Captain Frascatore, why did you permit this?' And I say 'I try to be kind to Mr. Finsch who is angry.' And they say —"

"But Captain," said Finsch in surprise, "I am not angry. I must merely show this puppy —"

"Come now, Mr. Finsch," said the captain in a conciliatory tone. "This is a trip for pleasure. You must relax. I will ask Mr. Bunpole to apologize for striking you. Then there will be no more trouble. What do you say? Come. Let us all have a drink."

Betty, Ora and Alec went back to the mess-hall, with Harry and Nello behind them. Harry Mayberry seated himself at the rummy game, picked up his cards. "My draw, I think."

"Yes," said Alec, "why not?"

Ora examined her cards. "We're lucky our doctors didn't send us on a sea voyage for rest."

A few moments later the captain entered the mess-hall. He darted a sour glance toward Betty, returned to the chess board. He looked around the room. "Where is Mr. Bunpole?"

No one knew.

The captain grunted, looked down at the board. "There must be no more of this trouble." His eyes glittered briefly toward Betty. "Everyone must cooperate."

"Don't blame me," snapped Betty. "I had nothing to do with this affair."

The captain grunted again; the chief engineer joined him and the chess game proceeded.

# 6

Betty sat quietly in the corner of the mess-hall. She had been invited into the rummy game, but declined, anxious only for passivity. She sat for half an hour almost in a torpor, lulled by the motion of the ship. Neither Finsch nor Ted showed themselves. Betty remembered that she had wanted to talk to Ted, but now she felt incapable of seeking him out. Where could he be? In bed? More likely he was off sulking by himself in the dark, taking the course most exactly calculated to irritate her. Why was he so dense? She puzzled about Ted. He's not stupid, he's not an introvert; he merely lacks the ability to see himself as others see him. Ted of course was not unique; no one ever exactly knew what sort of image they were creating in other people's brains. Covertly she inspected the four people playing cards. Four minds, four unique citadels full of private thoughts. How fascinating, this riddle of personality! Each one of these persons feels differently, sees life in different colors. Consider Harry Mayberry: a baby-pink satyr, or, by virtue of his gray tonsure, a derelict monk. Betty studied him, trying to see past the outward semblance which rather repelled her. He held his cards firmly, played decisively, without waste motion. That must mean something. Nello was full of flamboyant motion, snapping down the cards as if he were killing insects. He played recklessly and without calculation. A small matter, but Betty decided that she liked lecherous old Harry Mayberry more than handsome young Nello.

She turned her head to catch Alec's eyes on her, reminding her that she likewise was being judged, for better or worse, by signs, traits and mannerisms, of which, for the most part, she was unaware.

She thought of Ted...Where was that silly Ted? She heaved a sigh, deciding once more to find him and talk to him. She rose up on her knees, looked through the porthole out over the forward deck. The lights reflected on the glass and she could see nothing. It looked cold out there in the dark, and Betty sat down again. Damn Ted, all the trouble he's making!

She stirred herself, made an unobtrusive exit from the mess-hall. She paused in the corridor. The time was almost midnight; probably

Ted had gone to bed. Still, it would do no harm to take a walk forward, just in case Ted *was* martyring himself in the windy dark.

She went out on deck, groped her way to the bow, finding no one. For a few moments she stood enjoying the solitude and the motion of the bow, then returned shivering to the deck-house.

Ted evidently had retired. Betty was ready for bed herself; she'd look in on her way up.

She found her way to Ted's cabin, knocked on the door. As before, no response. As before, she opened the door, called, "Ted! Are you asleep?"

No answer.

Betty flicked on the light. The bed was the same: dent in the pillow, wrinkled counterpane. No change except...Betty entered the room quickly. On the pillow lay a piece of paper, folded over. Type-script read: MISS BETTY HAVERHILL.

She opened the paper with trembling fingers. The note read:

> *Dearest Darling:*
> *I have been a fool, and I have made a great deal of trouble. I cannot live without you, and so goodbye.*
>
> > *Yours forever,*
> > *Ted.*

# Chapter III

## 1

THE CAPTAIN PUT THE SHIP about, retraced the course at half-speed. The moon had set, the sea was dark as ink. Searchlights flitted over the surface like moths; everyone lined the rails, looking and listening.

After two hours the captain gave up the search, and the *Garda* resumed its course. The searchlights still swept back and forth over black water, crew and passengers kept lookout until the captain announced that they had reached the spot where Ted's absence had been discovered. There was no more hope, he said gruffly, and ordered the searchlights to be turned off.

Betty refused to go to bed and remained out on the wing of the flying bridge. The captain had refused to return back a second time, and Betty was bitterly angry.

"It is no use," he had barked. "There are currents, the water is cold. We have wasted much time already, and with a ship time is the same as money."

"Please don't shout at me," said Betty icily.

The captain shook his head in exasperation, swung on his heel and marched away.

Ora and Alec finally persuaded her down to the mess-hall. It was now four in the morning, and Alec took himself off to bed.

Two hours later the *Garda* reached the Port of Los Angeles. Bells tinkled between wheel-house and engine-room, a stillness came over the ship.

Betty and Ora went out on deck. The overcast still covered the sky, smothering the dawn, and sapping all color from land and sea. The ship barely moved through water that swirled and gleamed like aluminum paint. Beyond the break-water lay a gray waste of warehouses, oil-derricks and tanks.

A launch drew up to the side of the ship, the pilot came aboard. Telegraph bells tinkled; the *Garda* stirred and, picking up speed, drove through the break-water.

Half an hour later a tug nudged the ship against a dock. Lines were run ashore, winches rattled fore and aft, the *Garda* lay quiet.

Betty and Ora returned to the mess-hall, but it was cheerless in the gray daylight. "What will you do now?" asked Ora with unaccustomed diffidence.

"Go to bed, I suppose."

"I mean later."

Betty went to the porthole, looked out. There was little to see: the deck, the wharf, the side of a warehouse, two or three acres of sunburnt weeds, a freeway already busy with traffic. She turned away. "I'm not going home, if that's what you mean."

"You're perfectly right," said Ora. "After all, this thing isn't your fault."

"I still feel guilty." Tears came to her eyes as they had off and on all night. "Somehow...Well, never mind. Let's go to bed."

# 2

There was a knock at the door. Betty awoke with a startled jerk. She wrapped herself in her terry-cloth bathrobe, opened the door, to receive the news that the captain wished to see her in his cabin.

Betty dressed in a dark-green skirt and sweater, combed her hair listlessly. She felt tired and dull, and faintly sick to her stomach. Ted alive had been a bother and a nuisance, but Ted's death left an unpleasant gap in the universe. Almost as far back as she could recall Ted had been part of her environment. Now, no more Ted with stylish new clothes and his fancy-dan convertible.

In the captain's office were a number of men, who rose when she came in. The captain introduced them, but the names meant nothing. One was the Italian consul, another was a plain-clothes sergeant attached to the harbour police, two others were agents of the Mediterranean Line.

The captain was subdued and courteous. "I realize you are distressed; still we must make an official report regarding last night."

"Of course," said Betty. "I don't mind." The men were sympathetic, and seemed not to hold her responsible for Ted's insane act. They appeared interested in the farewell letter.

"Would you recognize Mr. Bunpole's handwriting?" asked the police official, a small dark man, with bright bird-like eyes, whose name was McElroy.

"I might. I don't know, for sure."

"Did he usually type personal communications — letters, notes, that sort of thing?"

"I don't know… I've never had a letter from Ted — before last night."

"Did you hear him threaten suicide last night?"

"No. I really can't believe it. He's always been so — well, normal. I know he was upset — but to throw himself in the ocean! It's absolutely weird."

"Strange things do happen. You read the note of course. What did you think of it?"

Betty stammered in bewilderment. "What did I think of it?"

"I mean, does it sound like Ted? Is this his phrasing?"

A sudden horrid suspicion came to Betty. She shrank back in her seat. "May I see the letter?" she asked huskily.

McElroy, holding it gingerly at the edges with his fingernails, said, "Please don't touch it."

Betty read the typewritten words:

*Dearest Darling:*
*I have been a fool, and I have made a great deal of trouble. I cannot live without you, and so goodbye.*

*Yours forever,*
*Ted.*

She shook her head. "I don't know. It sounds — strange."
McElroy nodded. "Not like Ted, eh?"

"Not really. He'd complain more — work himself into a fury. Then he'd feel sorry for himself and get drunk...I just can't understand Ted jumping into the ocean."

The captain moved uneasily. He started to speak, glanced significantly at the consul, who pursed his lips. The older of the agents said, "This is all supposition, of course."

McElroy nodded sourly. "When did you last see Ted?"

"The same time everybody else did, out on the hatch. Then after a while I went looking for him."

"How long after?"

"I don't know, really. Something like an hour, I suppose...Did anyone else see him after he left the hatch?"

"The officer on watch and the lookout both noticed him going forward to the bow. At least they saw a man in a light sweater — presumably Ted. The mate's not sure of the time. Somewhere after ten. That's the last we hear of him. Later they saw you go up and return...Is there anything else you can tell us, Miss Haverhill?"

Betty glanced at the captain, who regarded her with eyes like ball-bearings.

"I suppose Captain Frascatore told you about Ted fighting?"

"Yes." McElroy made no amplification.

Betty said rather feebly, "Well, I guess that's all I can tell you."

McElroy rose to his feet. "Thank you, Miss Haverhill. I think that's all we need. You intend to proceed with the ship?"

"Yes...But I'd better telephone my mother." Betty grimaced. "Can you tell me where to find a telephone?"

The younger agent jumped to his feet. "I'll show you. You'd never find it by yourself."

He led her to the main deck, down the gangway, through the warehouse. "This is a terrible shock for you," he said solicitously. "But you mustn't let it interfere with your trip."

"No," said Betty vaguely. "But I'm not really concerned about myself. It's Ted! A suicide! I still can't believe it!"

"Confidentially, I don't think anyone believes it. Except Captain Frascatore, who feels he must."

Betty looked at the agent more carefully. He was a stocky solid man in his middle thirties, with reddish-blond hair, a round well-meaning face. There was a nervous twitch to his lip, an apologetic droop to his eye; he wore a rumpled brown suit, a color exactly calculated to clash with his rusty-pink hair. A jaunty mustache decorated his lip, a brave symbol of the gallant and humorous man of action he considered himself.

"What will happen?" asked Betty.

The agent shrugged. "Probably nothing. Not now anyway. The ship is under Italian law. McElroy has no authority; he's investigating at the request of the consul. If he turns up proof of foul play — real proof — they might tie the ship up a few days. Otherwise —" he shrugged again.

"But surely there's suspicion, or at least the possibility —"

"That doesn't count for much."

Betty shuddered. "Poor Ted."

"You've got to remember that it costs money to operate a ship like the *Garda*," said the agent defensively. "Almost fifteen hundred dollars a day. The captain doesn't want to lie in port an hour longer than necessary… Incidentally, my wife is coming aboard the ship today. She'll be your room-mate." He paused, then said heartily, "She's a good sort; I know you'll get on together."

"I thought she was married to some man in San Salvador."

"Not San Salvador — El Salvador. El Salvador's the country, San Salvador's the capital city. But I'm still the man. I fly south tomorrow. Isabelle wants to come down to La Libertad but she can't stand airplanes."

They came to the telephone box; Betty approached the instrument with reluctance. She took a deep breath, and called home, collect.

Mother was stunned and horrified. "You're coming home, of course?"

"No, Mother."

"Why, Betty, that's the most —"

"Mother, I can't talk here. I called to let you know."

"Who'll tell Martha Bunpole?" cried Mother. "I won't be able to face her! I just can't do it!"

"The captain will probably call, or the police. It's not our responsibility. At least, it's not mine."

"You're absolutely heartless!"

"I'm no such thing! Now don't let's quarrel, Mother."

"I think you certainly should come home!"

"No, Mother. Now I'm going to hang up, because the ship leaves pretty soon. It's a terrible thing and I'm sorry, but Ted had no business coming on this trip."

"How can you *say* a thing like that!"

"Anyway I'm not going to come home. So now — take care of yourself, and don't worry!"

"You're a head-strong hard-hearted girl," said Mother in a cold quiet voice.

"I'm nothing of the sort. But I'm not a silly hysterical female, either."

"Very well, Betty. You must do as you think best."

Betty left the phone-booth feeling slightly less dismal. She had dreaded the call, but it hadn't been so bad. Poor Ted. It was the most shocking and tragic event of her life! But still — it had been no fault of hers. The disturbing speculation sidled into her mind. Could it possibly be... No, of course not. She turned to the agent. "What was your name?"

"Alan Calder. Isabelle is my wife. She'll be down this afternoon. The ship sails at six."

"You must know Mr. Finsch. He lives in El Salvador."

Calder nodded curtly. "Yes. I know Finsch. Know of him, at least."

"He's sold his plantation, or whatever it's called."

"I know."

"He seems to have had an interesting life," Betty ventured.

Calder said nothing.

They walked back to the ship. From the dock it looked enormous: bold black bow, the masts and booms, the deck-house. Alan Calder stopped abruptly at the bottom of the gangway, and stood scratching his mustache in desperate embarrassment. "I'd like to ask a favor of you," he said suddenly. "I know it's rather strange — I don't know you, you don't know me. It's about Isabelle. She's — well, just a little high-strung. Nice girl and all that, but — well, you'll be rooming with her." Alan Calder found it impossible to put his thoughts into words. He made a bluff reassuring gesture, grinned appealingly. "Forget what I said. You'll get along fine... I've got to run now."

"Thanks for showing me the phone," Betty called after him.

He gave his arm another jaunty flourish, jumped into one of the cars parked along the dock, drove hurriedly away.

# 3

Betty had missed both breakfast and lunch. Instead of returning aboard the ship she walked to a nearby lunch-wagon, ordered a hamburger and a milk-shake. The proprietor, mopping the counter, pointed down the wharf toward the *Garda*. "See that ship? One of the passengers jumped off last night, threw himself in the ocean. They never found him. What do you think of that?"

"It doesn't sound a very sensible thing to do."

"That's what I think. He must have been crazy to begin with, riding one of them old buckets."

"My mother thinks that way too," said Betty. She settled the check, wandered back down the dock to the ship, climbed the gangway.

From the galley came the rattle of pots and the smell of dinner. The crew's mess-hall rang to staccato Italian voices. From the engine-room came a slow hiss of idle boilers, a tapping of metal on metal. Home again, thought Betty.

None of the passengers were in evidence. Betty went up to her cabin, entered, locked the door, flung herself down on the bed, intending to take a nap before dinner.

But the thought of Ted kept her awake. Dreadful pictures passed through her mind: a body drifting through the depths, arms dangling, mouth hanging loose, opal eyes staring. Poor old Ted...Betty heaved a deep sigh. Suppose she had known he was planning such a thing? Would she have agreed to marry him?...There was the other possibility, the idea that McElroy had put into her mind, and which Alan Calder had more or less confirmed. Ted wasn't the sort to kill himself; it wasn't reasonable! She considered the note, the phrases, the typescript. Undoubtedly the authorities would examine it for fingerprints, but they'd find only her own. Not Ted's or anyone else's. What could they prove? Nothing; unless there were eye-witnesses — and if the event had taken place up at the bow, in the dark, who could have seen?

It was a ticklish situation. What should she do? Betty Haverhill, Private Eye. No, nothing like that. Probably there was nothing to detect. Probably Ted had jumped into the ocean of his own free will. They might never know…In any event, she'd had enough of gloom. All the moping in the world couldn't bring Ted back.

She freshened herself, and went up to the top deck. The Salvadorean ladies were playing quoits, with small skill but enormous enthusiasm. Alec and Ora, Harry Mayberry and Nello sat in deck-chairs under the awning, and a mess-boy was opening bottles of beer.

"Please don't move," said Betty as Harry Mayberry gallantly started to rise.

Harry Mayberry relaxed. "Would you like a bottle of beer?"

"Very much."

Alec regarded Betty thoughtfully through his pipe-smoke. "You're looking better, less wan, less pale."

"Miserable experience," murmured Harry Mayberry.

"I suppose they asked you all kinds of questions?" Alec inquired.

"Oh, yes. I told them everything I could."

"What did they seem to think?"

"I don't know. I suppose there's not much for them to go on."

"No."

The mess-boy arrived with more beer. Betty relaxed into the deck-chair, hoping to avoid more talk about Ted. Already he had receded, already he was part of the past. And this was the present, sitting on the deck of the *Garda*, drinking beer, looking over the wharf toward San Pedro. A taxi came bumping down the pier, stopped beside the ship. Alan Calder jumped briskly out, assisted a woman to the pier.

"Our new passenger," said Betty. "Her name is Isabelle."

# Chapter IV

## 1

Isabelle stood beside the cab, inspecting the *Garda*. She was blonde, slender, graceful. Alan Calder danced around her like a terrier, full of officious pride and solicitude.

Harry Mayberry made a soft yelping sound in his throat. "I'm in love."

"She's married," said the practical Nello.

"What's the difference?" Harry Mayberry rolled up his eyeballs. "She's human. If she's not, I'm going to change my nationality, or species, whatever you call it. If she's an ape, I'll be a woolly white ape. If she's a caterpillar, I'll crawl right after her. If she's a chicken, I'll fly the coop."

"If she's a goat," said Ora, "you can stay just as you are."

"She's certainly no goat," averred Alec. Ora looked at him in surprise. "You too?" She turned to inspect Isabelle once more. "What's she got that I haven't got?"

Betty felt a pang of something very similar to jealousy. There were now two pretty girls on the *Garda*. Isabelle was more than pretty. Her features were exquisite, composed and quiet, the face of a sullen fairy princess. Her hair was a pale tawny cream-color, and clung to her head like foam.

My new room-mate, thought Betty sourly. She felt less relaxed. Isabelle coming aboard meant competition, whether she wanted to compete or not. "The hell with it," Betty told herself. "She can be queen of the Pacific Ocean; I'm not going to trouble myself."

Isabelle noticed the group on the top deck. She gave them a casual glance, paid no further attention. A mess-boy came from the ship, took her suitcases. Alan solicitously led her to the gangway; they boarded the ship, passing out of sight under the boat deck.

Alec tapped his pipe against the rail. "An oddly-matched couple."

"Yes," said Ora reflectively. "How did he ever talk her into it? Is he rich?"

"You're cynical," said Betty. "Alan's very nice. He helped me find a telephone today."

Alec drained his glass of beer. "Something tells me that we'll remember the *Garda* a long long time."

Betty rose to her feet. "I'm going down to the cabin. She might want to know something."

Alan Calder and Isabelle had just entered the cabin when Betty appeared. Alan made a great show of hearty camaraderie. "Here you are! I've been telling Isabelle all about you! This is Betty Haverhill, darling."

Isabelle nodded, gave Betty a flicker of a smile. The wide gray eyes were observant but uninterested. Betty saw that she was not much older than herself—perhaps twenty-four or twenty-five.

"This is the bunk I've been sleeping on." Betty pointed. "This is my closet. It doesn't make much difference, they're both the same."

Isabelle nodded indifferently. "I'm not expecting too much."

"I'll leave you to sort yourself out," said Betty. "This cabin is rather small for three of us."

"It's small for two," said Isabelle. She gave Alan a brief glance. "But I guess there's no help for it."

"See you later," said Betty brightly, and backed out of the cabin. She returned to the top deck.

"Well?" asked Harry Mayberry. "How did you get along?"

"Very well."

"If you've got any objections to her, I'll trade her for Nello."

"I agree to that," said Nello.

Betty looked at her watch. "Six o'clock. We were scheduled to leave at six."

"They're still loading cargo," said Ora. "We'll be here hours yet."

"Have some more beer," said Harry Mayberry, proffering a half-empty bottle.

"Oh, all right."

Mik Finsch appeared on deck, came over to stand by the group. Betty stared fixedly into her glass of beer.

"An ugly harbor," said Finsch. "Most ports are ugly, but I think this is one of the worst possible. I do not like Los Angeles."

"It's an acquired taste," said Alec.

There was a short heavy silence.

"Yes," mused Finsch. "It will be pleasant to visit Europe again. I have not been there for twenty years. There will be many changes."

"Perhaps you'll be homesick for El Salvador," suggested Ora.

"No," said Finsch. "I am done with the tropics. No more. I have had enough. It is not good for a man." He raised his great arms, let them fall to his sides. The big thick-fingered hands, with black hair on the backs, hung only a yard from Betty's face.

There was another silence.

Finsch rubbed his face; his hand rasped on his chin. "I think I will shave before dinner. With so many ladies at hand, one must always be careful of his appearance."

"Don't trouble yourself on my account," said Ora drily.

"I will leave one third of my face unshaven," said Finsch politely. He strolled back across the deck, passed down the stairs and out of sight. Nello exhaled a deep sigh, Alec leaned back in his seat, Ora gave her head a vixenish toss. "Anyone want any more beer?" asked Harry Mayberry. "No? I don't want any more either. This Italian beer is not the best."

Ora rose to her feet. "It's almost time for dinner. I'm going below."

Betty followed her down the stairs, turned off into Cabin #2. Isabelle was not in evidence, although her four suitcases occupied the middle of the floor.

Betty washed her face, brushed her hair with vigorous strokes, touched lipstick to her mouth. Looking at herself in the mirror she felt dissatisfied with the dark-green sweater and changed into a striped black and white blouse. Ha, thought Betty sardonically, I'm not competing with my new room-mate. No. But I'm still not going down to dinner looking like a boy-scout.

She ran down the corridor toward the stairs. She thought of Ted (not twenty-four hours had passed; it seemed a week!) and slowed her steps. If Ted's spirit were hovering over the ship, she wouldn't want him to think her utterly heartless.

She reached the main deck. Along the corridor from the mess-hall came the sound of voices: the captain's jovial laugh, Alan Calder's baritone, coming in nervous volleys of syllables, like handfuls of pebbles against a window. She heard Finsch's rumble and Isabelle's bright tinkle. Evidently Ted had been forgotten: an incident of the voyage, sad, but best ignored.

Betty entered the mess-hall, halted. The captain and the chief engineer sat in their usual places, waiting for the dinner gong to sound. Directly across from the captain, in Harry Mayberry's place, sat Alan Calder. In Betty's place sat Isabelle, facing Mik Finsch. As Betty stood uncertainly, Alec and Ora came in through the opposite door, took their own places.

The captain noticed Betty. "Aha!" he told Isabelle. "Here is your room-mate. Two pretty girls in one cabin. Very nice. We do not have this often on the *Garda*. This is Miss Haverhill."

Isabelle glanced over her shoulder at Betty. "We've met."

Alan made a token attempt to rise, sank back in his chair. He looked nervous and tired, and watched Isabelle like a spaniel. When Isabelle looked at Alan she wore no expression whatever.

Betty fidgeted against the back wall. The dinner gong had not sounded; she could hardly ask Isabelle to move from her place. The captain noticed and raised his eyebrows in comprehension. He looked at Isabelle, back to Betty, rubbed his chin. "A new passenger. We must think about seating."

Isabelle shrugged her beautiful shoulders. "I don't care where I sit. I'm happy here, if no one else is disturbed."

The dinner bell rang; the Salvadorean ladies trooped in, took their places. Harry Mayberry strolled up behind Alan, so close that Alan had to lean forward to escape the protruding belly. "Excuse me. Am I in your place?" asked Alan. He moved to the table at the back of the room, where Ted Bunpole had sat. "Why don't you come back here, dear?" he called to Isabelle. "It's our last meal together for quite some time."

"Only ten days," said Isabelle flippantly. "And I'm all settled."

Betty flung herself into the seat across from Alan. She sulked over her soup. Alan Calder, half of his mind on the chatter at the front tables, manfully tried to be amusing, and Betty forced herself to be pleasant. There was one matter in which she was interested. "What's happening about Ted?"

"Ted? Ted Bunpole?" Alan Calder grimaced. "Miserable situation... I guess not much. There may be an investigation when the ship gets to Genoa — a crime aboard this ship is like a crime committed in Italy —"

"Crime?" asked Betty quickly. "They think it's a crime?"

Alan Calder rolled a bread-crumb between his fingers, threw it aside. "I meant in a general sense. Crime, accident, suicide, manslaughter. I don't know what's going to happen. Probably nothing."

"Poor Ted."

Alan Calder twisted the wine bottle so that the label faced him exactly, moved his fork, tugged at his necktie. "There's nothing to go on. Nobody's come forward with anything."

"I wish I knew," Betty muttered. "Knew, for certain!"

"That's just it. Speculation is one thing, accusation another."

The forward tables sounded to conversation in a more jocular vein.

"Finsch is selling his *finca*," the captain told Isabelle. "You should buy. You have plenty time. Then you and Alan can ride horses to look over your land."

"Wonderful," exclaimed Isabelle softly. "I love horseback riding."

"You see?" said the captain, spreading out his hands.

Alan straightened in his seat, shot his cuffs. "I don't have as much time as you think," he told the captain gruffly. "This business keeps me going. Don't forget, I've got Coyle and Dumas, Gorgas Lines, Pan-Pacific as well as Mediterranean." He darted a quick glance at Finsch. "Anyway Finsch has already sold out."

Finsch made an easy gesture. "It is true. I am finished with coffee. One hundred and twenty thousand dollars, that is what they paid me."

"That's a good price," said Alan.

Finsch nodded complacently. "Still it is a good property, if it is run correctly. There is much money to be made in coffee. More than in rubber."

"What will you do with all your money?" asked Isabelle in a teasing voice.

Finsch laughed. "I do not know. Perhaps I buy property. Perhaps I trade in fine jewels. I know certain people in Ceylon and Damascus and Istanbul. And one can buy diamonds very cheaply in Liberia. Who knows? Perhaps I give everything to the poor."

"You have no family?"

"No. No one."

"Why not a big motor launch in Tangiers?" suggested Nello brashly. "What do you say, Finsch? I'll go in with you. We run American cigarettes into Spain and Italy. Also nylons, antibiotics, whatever is short."

Finsch shrugged. "Why not? These are necessities, which people must use. It is no crime supplying them at a low cost."

Alan Calder gave a short bark of laughter which he hurriedly stifled. Isabelle turned a cool glance over her shoulder. Alan busied himself with the wine bottle.

An unlikely romance, thought Betty. How in the world had she come to marry him? Alan seemed a decent sort, but not at all Isabelle's type. "You're rather high-strung, aren't you?" asked Betty in a soothing voice.

Alan looked at her as if surprised by her perception. "I suppose I'm nervous — these days it's the occupational hazard to being alive." His eyes were dark hazel, restless as butterfly-wings. He'd be much more attractive, thought Betty, if he'd calm himself, keep his clothes in order, stop fiddling with everything within reach.

"You should come with us to El Salvador. The rest would do you good."

"I don't have time. I'm two days late as it is. I'd be a wreck. Too slow, much too slow."

"That's what I like," said Betty. "I'm in no hurry. How long does the *Garda* stay at La Libertad?"

"Depends on the cargo. Maybe a day, maybe two. Maybe only a few hours. La Libertad's not much to see, a typical tropical port, dirty as sin, hot as hell. You've got to go inland for scenery. Mountains, trees, flowers, rivers. San Salvador is a nice town, as Central America goes."

"San Salvador, El Salvador. I get them mixed."

"El Salvador's the country. San Salvador, that's the city. Don't ask me why. You should take a trip inland. It's picturesque, in spots. Also the lakes."

"I'd like to, but if we're only in port for a day —"

Alan made a careless gesture. "Leave the *Garda* at La Libertad, catch the *Maggiore* next month. You can see all Central America on your way to Europe."

"I didn't know I could do that."

"Certainly you can. If there's space available, and there usually is. If you want to wait over a month, see me at La Libertad."

"I'll probably go through on the *Garda*."

Alan gulped down his demi-tasse. "We'll talk about it in La Libertad. Excuse me." He swung around in the chair, rose to his feet, crossed the room to lean over Isabelle. "Finished, dear? It's only an hour till sailing time."

She looked up without expression. "I haven't even started my coffee."

"Hurry then, and we'll go topside."

"I don't want to stand out in that wind. I hate wind. If we've got to, let's go into the saloon, or lounge, whatever it's called."

"The lounge!" cried Alan with desperate gaiety. "You lounge in the deck-chairs! This is a freighter, not a sanitarium!"

Mik Finsch said humorously, "The *Garda* is not a floating palace, eh? No. I have ridden on many first-class ships. But the *Garda* will take us where we want to go."

"Exactly," said Alan. "It's a way to travel. I wish I could make the trip myself!"

Isabelle rose to her feet. "Let's go on top, then, if that's what you want."

Alan bustled forward, ushered her out the door. Betty felt a certain degree of sympathy for Isabelle. A husband like Alan could become an awful bother.

She left the mess-hall, and went forward to the bow, dodging through the longshoremen now covering the hatches. Here, to her faint surprise, she found Sergeant McElroy on his hands and knees, scrutinizing the deck.

"Detecting?" asked Betty in a brittle attempt at humor.

"I guess that's what it's called." McElroy rose to his feet. "Occasionally we find traces: fiber, skin, blood, oddments like that."

Betty looked around with a shudder. "You think it happened here?"

"Possibly. I don't know anything for sure."

"It's the most isolated spot on the ship."

"There are other possibilities. The area behind the life-boats, the fantail, the wings of the flying bridge."

"Have you learned anything new?" asked Betty diffidently.

McElroy shook his head. "Nothing very much. The mate saw someone in light clothes go forward and someone in light clothes come back. The lookout thinks he saw someone in dark clothes go forward. Naturally they weren't paying any particular attention."

"Ted was wearing a light-gray sweater. Does that mean —"

"All it means is that two persons went forward and one came back."

"But in that case —"

"It's inconclusive," said McElroy. "The captain is the only one who knows anything for sure. He says it's suicide. I can't contradict him. There's a fishy smell aboard this ship, but it might be only the bilge… That note, for instance."

"Yes. That note."

The ship's whistle first hissed, then blew, a long mournful blast.

McElroy heaved a sigh. "Well, it's about time for me to leave."

They returned down the deck. Betty asked, "Is this all the investigation there'll be?"

"It rather looks that way. Technically, it's the responsibility of the Italian authorities. Italy, of course, is ten thousand miles away. There's nothing much to go on."

"I wish I could think of something."

"An affair like this is hard to pin down. Ted might have jumped. Or he might have been knocked out and rolled over the side. I'd like to know. I've been in this business twenty years and I still get excited when somebody gets killed."

"I'd like to know too," said Betty grimly.

McElroy laughed. "Well, goodbye again, and have a pleasant trip."

"Thanks. Goodbye."

# 2

Yellow floodlights glared from the dock; the masts and booms cast crazy shadows across the hatches. A tug nosed up to the bow; deck-hands sent down a hawser which was made fast to a bitt on the deck of the tug. Shore lines were cast off; the tug churned up water, and a line of darkness separated the ship from the dock. The telegraph tinkled, the engine throbbed, the *Garda* moved out into the stream.

Betty, Alec and Ora, Nello and Harry Mayberry sat in deck-chairs along the rail, watching the lights of Long Beach dwindle across the water. For no particular reason Betty began to cry. Tears ran down her cheeks, while she apologized in embarrassment.

"It's normal," said Ora. "A release of bottled-up tension."

Betty wiped her eyes with the back of her hand. "I don't know what came over me. It's the ocean, I suppose — so dark and sad, with all the pretty lights falling astern."

"The dark ocean," said Alec solemnly. "A very powerful symbol — equivalent to death."

Ora made a disgusted noise.

"Scoff as you will, it's the truth," said Alec.

Betty laughed mournfully. "You're at least partly right. I saw the ocean and I thought of Ted."

After a short silence, Harry Mayberry said speculatively, "I wonder how Comrade Finsch is amusing himself tonight?"

"He's in the mess-hall," replied Nello in a gay voice. "He and Isabelle are drinking cognac."

"I was planning to buy her a drink myself," said Harry Mayberry. "Now I don't think I will."

"Ah — you don't like competition?"

"I want to make the trip."

The *Garda* slid south past the shore cities: Seal Beach, Hermosa Beach, Laguna Beach. At eleven-thirty Alec and Ora went below. Harry Mayberry began yawning and lurched to his feet. Nello hopefully remained seated, but Betty, who was not particularly fond of Nello, said goodnight and went below too.

Isabelle was already in bed, smoking a cigarette and reading the *New Yorker*. The porthole was closed; the cabin seemed exceedingly hot and stuffy.

Isabelle looked up, nodded, returned to her magazine. "Don't you think it's warm in here?" asked Betty tentatively. "Perhaps we could open the porthole."

"I'm just getting over a cold," said Isabelle. "I don't dare sit in a draft."

Betty flung off her clothes, washed her face, lay down on the bed. Sweat oozed from her skin, the sheets felt sticky. Finally she fell asleep, drugged by the heat, hypnotized by the thud of the engines.

# 3

Betty awoke with a headache, her eyelids thick and heavy as shingles. She lay torpidly for five minutes, then in a kind of frenzy, threw herself out of bed. "I've got to get out of this smelly cabin!"

She rinsed her face with cold water, brushed her teeth; she thought of the shower, but the time was seven-twenty. Breakfast in ten minutes. Isabelle still lay dozing, a bronze arm stretched artlessly across her face.

Betty slipped into jeans, a blouse and sandals, tied her hair into a pony-tail. Isabelle, now awake, watched dispassionately.

"Breakfast in about five minutes," said Betty.

"This is the earliest I've been awake for ages," said Isabelle. "I love to sleep."

"There's not much else to do," said Betty. "Sleep and eat and read."

Isabelle's ice-gray eyes were speculative. "I hear your boyfriend jumped over the side on the way down from San Francisco."

"Yes. He jumped or — fell."

"People who fall don't leave notes."

"People who jump don't use typewriters." Betty went to the door. "See you below."

"Righto." Isabelle threw her slender legs over the side of the bed. Betty left the cabin.

Down in the mess-hall she halted. Where should she sit? In her old place, or at the table to the rear?

Rats, said Betty, devil take the hindmost. She seated herself in her old place beside Alec.

Alec raised his eyebrows. "Good morning. Sleep well?"

"Well enough. Where's Ora?"

"She'll be down. You and I are early this morning."

Aside from the Salvadorean ladies, always prompt to their meals, they were the only passengers in the mess-hall.

Ora presently arrived, and Harry Mayberry and Nello. The little table at the rear of the mess-hall began to seem conspicuous. I'm making a fool of myself, thought Betty: people who go around asserting their rights always end up hot and undignified. On the other hand, nice guys come in last.

Isabelle came into the mess-hall, wearing black toreador pants and a turquoise sweater. She stopped short. Betty felt ice-gray eyes playing on the back of her neck.

Isabelle modestly seated herself at the back table. Betty felt hot and uncomfortable. The victory — if it were a victory — was a hollow one.

Mik Finsch ambled into the mess-hall, wearing white linen slacks, a short-sleeved white shirt. He stopped beside the back table, and spoke in a voice of humorous solicitude. "How pathetic. Alone, solitary, a poor lost little child. We cannot allow this. If you permit, I will join you."

Isabelle flashed up a quick glance which seemed to answer Finsch's question. He settled himself into the chair opposite Isabelle, and the seating arrangements had shifted again, evidently to their lowest center of gravity.

# 4

When the passengers went up to the top deck, there were blue patches in the overcast. The prospect of sunlight put everyone in good spirits. The Salvadorean ladies tossed quoits with volubility and excitement. Harry Mayberry pointed out imaginary black flying fish to Nello. "Look, there…You missed him. You're not quick enough. There's another, black as sin…"

Alec and Ora argued about the exact color of Ora's hair. "Words are words and hair is hair," said Ora impatiently. "What difference does it make?"

"You miss the point. Words are the raw material of poetry, and of all the art-forms poetry is the most expressive. Sausage-red, barn-red. These are poetic images."

"Damn the poetry. Sing your poems elsewhere. Plain red is good enough."

"Shrimp-cocktail red... Sunburn-red... Rhode Island Red."

"Really Alec," said Betty, "you're not at all kind."

Ora laughed bitterly. "He called me Reynard the first two years we were married."

Nello tugged at Betty's pony-tail. "What of this? An amazing creation, don't you think."

"Nello, please stop mauling me."

"Nothing is as decadent as fashion," declared Nello. "Men's fashion, women's fashion. Think how many parasites are supported by such as this!" He pointed to the pony-tail. "The communist countries have outlawed it, together with jazz music and Coca-Cola. In Russia they would do so." He took hold of the pony-tail and pretended to clip it.

Betty removed Nello's fingers. "Since we're capitalists, we can wear our hair any way we like."

"Don't call me that name!" Nello said staunchly. "I am no capitalist."

"No?" asked Harry Mayberry. "What are you then? A Methodist?"

"I am a Communist," said Nello with dignity. "Like every man with a conscience."

"That's why Nello is so modest about his title," chuckled Harry Mayberry. "He doesn't want to be mistaken for an aristocrat."

"Nello's an aristocratic Communist," said Betty.

Nello shook his handsome head. "You laugh at me but I have seen things you would never believe, if I talked an hour. In India, there are people who will do anything, absolutely anything, for a rupee or two."

"Even less, Nello tells me, if you haggle a bit," said Harry Mayberry.

"The world is changing, falling around your feet," Nello warned. "The dinosaurs are extinct, the feudal barons —"

"Speak of the devil," murmured Ora, as Mik Finsch appeared on deck. He nodded placidly to those in the deck-chairs, went forward to the wing of the flying bridge.

Harry Mayberry turned to Betty. "Where's your beautiful room-mate?"

"I don't know. I have trouble enough remembering where I am myself."

Five minutes later Isabelle appeared on deck. She had changed her sweater for a strapless black halter. She paused under the awning, exchanged a few polite remarks with Alec and Nello, ignoring Betty, Ora and Harry Mayberry. Then she settled herself across the deck and began to read her *New Yorker*.

Finsch paced sedately back and forth across the flying bridge. He paused on the starboard wing to inspect the sky, to blow a thoughtful plume of cigar smoke toward the horizon. He turned, crossed to the port wing, stood contemplating the parched hills of Lower California. His inspection seemed to satisfy him; he nodded, turned away; to his surprise there was the deck-chair in which Isabelle Calder reclined.

"Aha," said Finsch. "The overcast is lifting."

"So it is," said Isabelle.

"Your husband," said Finsch, his half-smile arch and mischievous, "would he object if I talked to you?"

"I imagine he would."

Finsch drew up a deck-chair. "Alan makes a mistake allowing his beautiful wife to travel alone."

"He warned me against unscrupulous men," said Isabelle. "I laughed at him. Scrupulous people are always so dull; Alan's so scrupulous he embarrasses me."

Finsch appeared to ponder. "Am I scrupulous? Or unscrupulous? I do not know. It is a matter which does not worry me. In any event I hope I should never embarrass you."

Isabelle pointed her toes demurely. "Thank you very much."

Betty watched from across the deck. Isabelle rolled her magazine into a tight cylinder, tapped it against her hip as she talked. Her ice-gray eyes shone, her air of sullen dissatisfaction had evaporated. A woman of moods, thought Betty. Finsch also seemed to be enjoying himself. Betty sneered inwardly. Jealousy? Of course not! She was pleased that Finsch had found something to distract his attention. It's just that — well...Well, what? Betty considered herself. Blue jeans, plaid blouse, pony-tail. She reviewed her wardrobe. Gray jersey dress: too hot. White shorts, white polo-shirt. Better — but still not like Isabelle in her tight black pants. I'll just ignore them both, thought Betty. Competition is ridiculous. Even if you won, what was the prize? Finsch?

# 5

Lunch was over: *antipasto*, *cannelloni*, a salad of watercress and cucumber, chicken *cacciatore*, roast beef. Isabelle yawned and stretched. "I simply must unpack, but all I want to do is sleep."

"I have few possessions," said Finsch. "In an hour I am ready to leave for any part of the world."

"Heavens!" exclaimed Isabelle prettily. "It takes me a week just to work up enough energy. I'm a very lazy person!"

"I too am lazy," said Finsch. "But I have worked hard in my life. God! How I have worked! But no more." He struck a match to his after-lunch cigar. "It is over, the work. Now others must work for me."

"That's great," said Harry Mayberry from the center table. "If you can make it stick."

"Why not?" asked Finsch. "I know many beautiful places where the best things of life can be found. In Madeira, in Majorca, in Istanbul, even a poor man may live in comfort, and I am not a poor man."

"You're lucky," said Isabelle. "I haven't travelled much. Alan makes El Salvador sound like Shangri-La."

Finsch puffed his cigar, but said nothing. Betty felt a trace of pity for Isabelle. Alan evidently had painted a highly romantic picture. How had he described La Libertad? "— a typical tropical port, dirty as sin, hot as hell." Isabelle was in for a shock. No wonder Alan felt nervous.

Isabelle excused herself and left the mess-hall. Finsch belched quietly, puffed his cigar, put his hands flat on the table. "I think I too will rest. But first, a turn around the deck to settle one's lunch, that is best." He pulled himself to his feet, sauntered out into the passageway.

There were a few moments of thoughtful silence.

"I think," said Harry Mayberry, looking off into space, "I think that there's dirty work at the crossroads."

"Ah?" asked Alec delicately.

"I can smell it. You can't fool an old pro. Nothing's started yet, of course."

Betty's cheeks began to burn, as she remembered her own small affair with Mik Finsch. She wondered if Harry had diagnosed 'dirty work at the crossroads' in her case too. The idea annoyed her to such an extent that she took issue with him: "She only said goodbye to her husband last night; she'll see him in a week!"

Harry Mayberry turned her a glance so knowledgeable, so cynical and lewd, that Betty held her tongue.

# Chapter V

## 1

THE *GARDA* WAS FIVE DAYS out of Los Angeles, half-way to La Libertad. The mountains of Jalisco reared like broken tiles ten miles to the east. The sea shone like soapstone, the weather was hot, the sky cloudless, but pale and hazy.

After five days Betty felt as if she had known no other home. Her fellow passengers? The circumstances intensified their characteristics as water brings out the color of dry rock. Betty thought them the most unique persons alive. In a letter to her Aunt Ethel she essayed a series of thumb-nail character-studies. Then she wrote:

> *These are the people in my life. As you will notice, I'm*
> *not equally enthusiastic about all of them. Mik Finsch and*
> *Isabelle have established a clique, membership limited to two.*
> *The rest of us naturally suspect the worst.*
> *The effect of Ted's disappearance — suicide I suppose we*
> *should call it — is gradually wearing off. Already it seems*
> *years and years ago — the effect of this shipboard existence.*
> *I still can't believe it happened. It seems absolutely unreal.*
> *I suppose it's real enough for poor Ted. Aside from Ted and*
> *my temperamental blonde room-mate, things are pleasant*
> *enough. If I didn't feel vaguely guilty about Ted — but I refuse*
> *to any longer. It wasn't my fault, and I'm not going to talk*
> *myself into some imaginary bereavement. Don't think I'm*
> *callous; it's just that life must go on, and Ted meant nothing*
> *to me in the first place. It still seems strange, but there's no*

*use thinking about it. It might even have been some kind of accident. Well, enough of Ted. I won't mention him again. Isabelle leaves the ship at La Libertad. How I wish she'd take Mik Finsch with her! But since her husband will be there to meet her, I suppose that's out.*

*I sleep ten to twenty hours a day, and I fear I'm gaining weight. The ship plugs along at a steady eleven knots, there's sun by the bucketful and I'm already the color of a well-done waffle. So, until next time…*

Betty signed her name, re-read the letter. She had written much, omitted much more. Licking the envelope, she glanced across the deck, to where Isabelle Calder, in the briefest of black shorts and a halter only slightly larger than a pair of sun-glasses, sunned herself. Her color was even more delicious than Betty's own. Finsch was below, sleeping off his lunch, according to his invariable routine. Betty covertly inspected Isabelle. Her face in repose was sweet and child-like. How had nervous perspiring Alan Calder ever persuaded her to become his wife? It was a source of unending wonder.

In one particular Isabelle was the ideal room-mate: she was quiet. She seldom if ever spoke, she left Betty entirely alone. The competition which Betty apprehended failed to materialize, since Isabelle acted as if she had already won. Betty felt mingled annoyance and relief. Finsch's animal magnetism, like the magnetism of iron, had polarity: it repelled as well as attracted. Betty now felt only revulsion for Mik Finsch. Still he had terminated his attentions toward her with embarrassing abruptness. Vanity, vanity! thought Betty. She gave Isabelle another surreptitious inspection, assessing, comparing. They were of an identical size, with the same rounded slender figures, and both were tawny from the sun. There the resemblance ended. Betty's features were casual and irregular, given charm by her air of happy-go-lucky generosity. Isabelle's face was perfect, and she flaunted an insolent vivacity. She would always photograph well, whereas Betty, inspecting snapshots, often felt herself the victim of a cruel practical joke.

Isabelle turned her head, and found Betty staring at her. She raised her eyebrows the width of a molecule, settled herself once more. But the sun was hot, and Isabelle decided that she had baked herself sufficiently. She rose to her feet, crossed the deck, disappeared below.

I'll remember this trip a long time, thought Betty. And it's hardly started. But if I can stand it another five days... A sudden thought struck her. After sunbathing, Isabelle showered. Betty jumped up as if she had been stung. She ran below.

Too late. From the shower came the sound of rushing water. Betty's clean towel was nowhere to be seen. Isabelle's towel lay in the corner, wet and trampled where she had kicked it after her morning shower.

Betty seated herself on the bed. Five more days. On the night after Isabelle's debarkation, she would buy champagne... But Mik Finsch would still be aboard. Betty prayed. Please God, make them get off together!

# 2

In her letter Betty had written much and omitted much. Tapping the letter against her fingers, Betty considered the events of the last five days. Without Isabelle the trip would have been a pleasure. Even the presence of Finsch could have been supported — because after all, one did not have to room with Finsch.

Betty tried to be fair. Perhaps there was offense in both directions, perhaps she was as guilty as Isabelle... No. Betty put the idea aside. No one could be as offensive as Isabelle. Resenting the necessity of sharing a cabin, Isabelle had arranged matters to suit herself. If Betty objected, she could follow Ted over the side: such was the implication of Isabelle's petulant shrug. To begin with, there had been the altercation over the porthole. The first night Isabelle had her way, and the porthole remained closed. The second night was warmer than the first. Betty's temper was already strained, because Isabelle, showering for the third time, had borrowed Betty's towel. When Betty came to go to bed, the porthole was closed, the room was thick with the odor of cigarettes, perfume, human breath, damp towels.

Betty stood in the doorway, and spoke in a hushed and wondering voice, "How can you live? It's stifling!"

Isabelle glanced briefly up from her magazine. She looked fresh as a lily. "You must have a high metabolism. It's just comfortable in here."

"I can't stand it. We've simply got to get some air."

Isabelle shivered. "There's a terribly cold wind tonight. I hate wind."

"Why don't you get under the covers?" asked Betty. "I'll give you my blanket."

Isabelle pretended not to hear.

Betty said, "I hope you roast," and left the room.

She stalked furiously down to the mess-hall. Here she found Mik Finsch and Harry Mayberry introducing Nello to the game of draw poker. Betty sat down to watch, and presently found herself acting as Nello's advisor.

The game did not end happily. At one o'clock Betty soberly mounted the stairs, her mind so full of Mik Finsch that Isabelle's obstinacy seemed of small concern.

She opened the door quietly, partly from consideration, and partly because she planned to achieve by stealth what she had failed to win by protest. Isabelle might die of pneumonia; nevertheless there had to be air in the room. Betty hooked the door open, drew the curtain provided for the purpose across the opening. There was a small rattle of curtain rings. Isabelle raised on her elbow. "What are you doing?"

"I'm letting some air into the room."

Isabelle said fretfully, "I can't sleep with half the crew peering in at me."

"I don't like it either," said Betty reasonably. "But it's better than smothering."

Isabelle flung herself back on her pillow. "Damnation...Open the porthole if you've got to."

"It's a warm night."

"Rmmf."

Betty closed the door, raised the porthole. She undressed, climbed into bed. The sheets smelled of stale tobacco. Betty sighed. For the first time she wondered whether ten days of Isabelle might not prove unendurable. She had expected small irritations...Make the best of things — hazards of travel — ten days, only eight more...

Betty awoke with a headache. The porthole, clamped shut, admitted light the color of milky water.

Betty dragged her legs out of bed, sat up. She groped for her watch, focused on the dial with difficulty. Six-thirty. Isabelle stirred and awoke, looking fresh and cool.

"Good morning," said Betty in a neutral voice.

"Good morning," said Isabelle.

Eight more days, thought Betty. God give her strength! It was bound to get worse before it got better.

# 3

During the day the weather became so hot that the porthole was left open without further controversy. But with the rise of temperature, Isabelle began to shower with ever more frequency — on awakening, before lunch, after sunning, before dinner, before retiring, whenever the impulse came over her. For her first one or two showers Isabelle used her own towel, and afterwards absent-mindedly took Betty's. When Betty went to take her own shower, there was nothing available but a wad of dank cloth. After the second such occurrence Betty displayed her towel to Isabelle. "I'm putting my towel here — on this hook. This is your towel here — so there won't be any mistakes!"

Isabelle nodded without particular interest, and for the third day in succession … Betty said crossly, "Please, Isabelle, won't you try to manage with your own towel? Every time I reach for mine you've already used it."

"I suppose I am a bother," said Isabelle with unconvincing contrition. "But then — there's no harm done. Nothing to fuss about. Ring for the steward. He'll bring towels by the armful."

"That's just exactly the point," said Betty. "He brings me one towel every day. I need only one. Why don't you make some kind of arrangement with him? Have him leave you two or three towels?"

Isabelle sniffed and shrugged. "That's just what they're waiting for. When you ask favors, they expect tips. It's not that I'm stingy, but I think they should do their jobs without holding their hands out."

Leaving Betty sitting wordlessly on the bed, she sauntered forth to meet Mik Finsch.

On the fourth day Betty folded her towel, put it away in her closet, and had the satisfaction of knowing that Isabelle hated her.

On the fifth day Betty wrote her letter to Aunt Ethel. Bruno, the steward, was late making up the rooms, and Betty forgot to take precautions. In need of a fresh towel, Isabelle had taken the first at hand.

By this time Betty had arrived at some understanding of Isabelle's thought-processes. She returned to the top deck, her rage mixed with amusement. Isabelle used her frontal lobes as little as possible, preferring to be guided by impulses of the last moment. Past and future were vague to Isabelle, but in compensation, the present was superlatively vivid. She enjoyed with exhilaration, she disliked with detestation. Isabelle could not abide the sensation of stickiness: she must shower. Isabelle needed a towel. There was a selection of two, the first limp and wet, the second clean and dry. Easily predictable was the towel upon which Isabelle's hand would fall. Complaints? They could be dealt with later, or ignored... Betty heaved a deep sigh. In this case *tout comprendre* was not *tout pardonner*. But it must be borne. There was nothing else to do. Only five more days and Isabelle would be no more than a memory.

Mik Finsch came up the stairs, first the top of his broad-brimmed hat appearing; then his dark blunt-featured head; then his massive shoulders and thick torso in a short-sleeved blue shirt; then his hips in tan shorts and his bare muscular legs; finally, his feet in white sneakers. He nodded at Betty with great affability, settled himself with a lurch and a grunt in the shade, lighted a cigar, drew on it with enormous gusto.

Betty watched him from the corner of her eye. In her letter she had hinted of the camaraderie which had sprung up between Isabelle and Finsch, but had provided none of the racy details. There was a quality to the situation — a facility, a boldness, a lack of embarrassment — which Betty found peculiarly shocking. Neither seemed to care a fig for the opinions of the other passengers, though they conducted themselves with perfunctory discretion while sitting on deck. As soon as Isabelle appeared, Finsch would amble up, the smoke from his cigar trailing a rich aroma downwind. They would draw deck-chairs together, and talk with animation and enjoyment. Finsch's half-smile would broaden into a heavy grin; Isabelle's features would take on a vitality which seemed to be reserved for this sort of occasion; she would tilt her head, purse her mouth, arch her eyebrows, twist her hips provocatively.

Finsch did most of the talking, discoursing in long measured sentences, or propounding massive jocularities which seemed to please Isabelle, for her laughter would tinkle across the deck. Occasionally she would sit erect in her chair in sudden excitement, to challenge, refute or tease. To all intents and purposes, they cruised aboard their private yacht, ignoring the other passengers. When the sun penetrated under the awning, they moved across the deck to a cooler spot, sometimes settling directly over Cabin #2.

This gave rise to a peculiar and momentous situation. Into the ceiling of each cabin below opened a ventilator, protected from the weather by a low mushroom cap. These steel mushrooms grew everywhere on the top deck. No one gave them a thought — except Betty. For on two occasions she found herself in the cabin while Finsch and Isabelle Calder sat directly above. Every word they spoke was transmitted down the ventilator, faintly but with unnatural clarity. On the first occasion Betty was uncomfortable and embarrassed; on the second occasion she was horrified.

Sometimes Finsch and Isabelle strolled forward to the bow, to watch flying fish or porpoise. Sometimes they sat in the mess-hall with a bottle of beer, or a glass of cognac. Sometimes they disappeared and Betty might not see them for hours. Sometimes Alec or Ora, or Harry, or Nello might disappear, but she always knew where they were and what they were doing. When Finsch and Isabelle disappeared, Betty likewise knew pretty well where they were and what they were doing.

Across the deck Finsch took off his hat, fanned himself with it. He took the cigar from his mouth, inspected it with approval, put it back, drew a long rich draught, let the smoke ooze slowly from his mouth. A revolting man, thought Betty. Fascinating to look at, of course, with his big dark face and his sphinx-like smile. But he was not likeable, not at all. Under his mask of affability he was dark and fierce and secretive. He was a wretchedly poor sport. Betty's mind went to the poker game of the second night out. Nello, through ignorance of the game, had been losing; then Betty began helping him, and Nello began to win: slowly at first, then faster — pots of fifteen cents, twenty-five cents, sixty cents on a full-house against Finsch's three aces.

As the coins stacked up in front of Nello, Finsch's joviality soured. His grin became mirthless, his eyes went opaque. After Nello's sixty-cent pot, Harry Mayberry and Finsch both won small hands; then Nello filled a straight and took another fifty cents.

Harry Mayberry threw up his hands. "I've had it!"

"Are you quitting?" asked Finsch.

"I'm cleaned out, unless I break a twenty, which I don't want to do. I know when I'm licked; it happens so often."

"Beginner's luck," rumbled Finsch. He hitched himself closer to the table. "We cannot stop now. I am behind."

"That's the way it always is," said Betty. "It's the theory of the game. Somebody wins, somebody loses."

"Usually me," said Harry Mayberry. "I'm glad to have company."

"We are not finished yet," said Finsch, looking earnestly from face to face. "I am behind three dollars and forty-one cents."

"Oh very well," said Harry Mayberry. He turned to Nello. "Lend me a dollar or two."

"Why not?" said Nello in high good spirits. "Here — two dollars."

Finsch took a large black wallet from his inside pocket, withdrew two five-dollar bills. "Now, we play."

On the first hand, he carefully inspected his cards, opened for fifty cents.

"Ouch!" muttered Harry Mayberry. "That's rather healthy."

"Now we play," said Finsch.

Nello's hand showed only a pair of tens. Betty nudged him to throw in, but Nello, encouraged by his run of luck, ignored her. He tossed fifty cents into the pot. Harry dropped out. Finsch drew two cards, Nello drew three. He failed to help himself, and took no pains to conceal his disappointment. Watching Finsch, Betty saw his gaze drop to his own cards, felt rather than saw him come to a decision. With ominous deliberation he pushed a dollar into the pot. Nello was dampened. He started to throw in his hand, but Betty reached past him. "A dollar, and raise two dollars."

Finsch's grin broadened, his teeth glittered. "Very well. Two dollars, and two dollars again."

"I thought we were only amusing ourselves," Harry Mayberry protested.

"I am very amused," said Finsch.

"I'm amused," said Betty cheerfully. "Another two dollars? And we raise —" she counted "— two dollars and sixty-seven cents — all we have."

"Two dollars and sixty-seven cents," Finsch repeated in a voice like the tolling of a bell. "I raise ten dollars."

"You can't," Harry Mayberry told him. "All you can do is call."

Finsch turned his great head slowly toward Harry. "I don't play such nonsense."

Harry shrugged. "Those are the rules. Bets are limited to money on the table. When a man shoots his wad, the other man calls him or folds. Otherwise millionaires would win every pot."

Finsch nodded slowly. "Very well, I must call."

Nello hesitated, diffident about displaying his pair of tens. Betty took the cards from his hand, spread them on the table. "A pair of tens," she said cheerfully. "What do you have?"

Finsch nodded again, carefully, tucked his hand into the deck. "You are very clever. But it is not the way I play."

"We didn't want your coffee plantation," said Betty, "so we let you off the hook."

"Thank you," said Finsch. "Although I no longer own a coffee plantation…Well, that is enough for tonight."

"No," exclaimed Nello. "Now we drink brandy. I have a liter in my cabin."

"Good," said Finsch. "I will drink a brandy."

Nello went after his bottle, and Betty stood up. "I'm going to bed. Goodnight everybody."

"Come back here, cherub," said Harry Mayberry, and tried to catch hold of her, but Betty dodged and ran up the stairs to bed.

The next day Harry Mayberry mourned his hangover, Nello was unusually quiet, and Finsch was his affable self. Betty eventually learned from Harry that over the bottle of cognac the game recommenced. Finsch had won back his money, as well as twenty-two dollars more.

Betty repressed her first comment. She said, "Maybe Nello's learned a lesson."

"So have I," said Harry Mayberry. "I like a friendly game — whether I win or lose."

"Some people can't stand losing," said Betty.

"At least Nello only lost his money," said Harry.

This had happened three days ago. Sitting on the deck, watching Finsch from the corner of her eye, Betty wondered what would happen when Finsch lost Isabelle at La Libertad.

Light was cast on the matter three days later, with the ship only thirty-six hours out of La Libertad. The news came via the ventilator — the second time that Betty had been an unwitting eavesdropper. The first time had been the morning after the *Garda* entered the tropics, slanting southeast past barren Cape Falso at the tip of Baja California. The time was ten o'clock; Betty sat on her bed sewing the zipper of her shorts. From far away came the sound of voices. Betty paid no particular attention; there were always voices to be heard somewhere on the ship. These particular voices, although faint, were astonishingly clear. Betty subconsciously noted Finsch's rumble and Isabelle's tinkling soprano. Then a word of universal import penetrated her attention: "— money." It was Isabelle's voice, faint and thin like fairy speech. "He spent three thousand on my operation, and it's all he talks of. I detest that kind of man. Always knows how much money he's carrying, to the cent."

Isabelle apparently was discussing her husband — who else? She seemed not to know that Finsch had already become notorious as the thriftiest man aboard the ship.

From the ventilator came Finsch's heavy baritone, less clear than Isabelle's voice, but it seemed to be a question, something like: "A three thousand dollar operation? That is a great deal of money."

"Yes," said Isabelle prettily. "But aren't I worth it?"

"Oh more, much more." Then Finsch said something which made Betty squirm with embarrassment, but which seemed to delight Isabelle, for she laughed her silvery laugh.

Then Finsch asked another question — something about the operation. Isabelle's laugh stopped short. There was an almost imperceptible hesitation, then Isabelle said, "My sinuses. They were twisted like corkscrews. It was an awful job. You can barely see the scar."

"Oh yes. Yes indeed."

Betty finished her sewing. The conversation held a kind of unpleasant fascination, but she put on her shorts and the stir of her movement overcame the faint sound of conversation.

This was the first time she overheard Mik Finsch and Isabelle. The second occasion occurred four days later, under almost identical circumstances. The time again was ten o'clock in the morning. Betty had gone into Cabin #2 to change the film in her camera. From overhead came the voices. Betty listened, half in shame, half in frank interest. They sat closer to the ventilator; the voices were more distinct. Isabelle was complaining of the heat. "I never imagined I could be so hot! I just got out of the shower and I'm all over sticky already!"

"Heat is a characteristic of the tropics," said Finsch with complete seriousness. "This is nothing. El Salvador is far more hot."

"If for no other reason, I'm not getting off," said Isabelle. Betty blinked. "I don't know what Alan was thinking of, telling me San Salvador was like Los Angeles."

"San Salvador is more cool than La Libertad, that is true," Finsch conceded. "It is more high, there is more wind. But to say it is cool — no."

"Alan would swear it was like Labrador to get me down there. He saved a hundred dollars sending me down on this ratty old tub — oh, the stories he told! Exquisite food! I can't touch half that slop. Cabins built for a queen! And I'm stuck in with that silly girl, and I'll be stuck with her clear across to Italy."

"No matter," said Finsch. "It is done, and now we are happy for Alan's tricks. It was to our benefit. You will see Paris, Brussels, Amsterdam: excellent places. The finest music, the best restaurants. You will eat such food as you never have before!"

"You don't want me to get fat, do you?" Isabelle asked in a teasing voice. "When I get fat I get lazy."

"I will see that you do not get fat. You will have much exercise."

"More than now?"

"One can hope."

Betty sat down on the bed. Instead of another day and a half of Isabelle, there was to be three more weeks! She stared at the ceiling. Three more weeks!

# CHAPTER VI

## 1

THE *GARDA* HAD COME a long way: down through the gray-green waters under the California overcast, along the parched coast of Lower California, past Cape Falso and across the mouth of the Gulf of California to Cape Corrientes; past Acapulco by night, with neon signs blinking; across the uncertain Gulf of Tehuantepec, then back close to the coast, now verdant and inviting, with great mountains rising behind the beaches. At twilight, off the coast of Guatemala, the *Garda* ran into a fantastic display of lightning, bolts like the roots of a tree fracturing a wet black velvet sky. The dwarfed *Garda*, slow as a minute-hand, drew out from under and left the splintering light and rumbling sound astern — farther and ever farther, until only a flickering at the north horizon remained.

The night of lightning was the ninth, less than twenty-four hours from La Libertad. Betty enjoyed the evening tremendously — because in twenty-four hours she, Isabelle and Mik Finsch would part ways forever.

Until noon of the ninth day Betty had sat staring at the sea, paralyzed with despair. After nine days she disliked Isabelle more than anyone she had ever known. It was an effort to go to bed at night, because then she must look at Isabelle, breathe the same air, smell Isabelle's perfume, her cigarettes, her soiled underclothes. (Isabelle, infinitely meticulous with the clothes on her back, lost interest once they had been used, and let them accumulate in a corner.) For nine days Betty had counted the hours, and then, instead of one more day, there were to be two and a half more weeks!

The problem solved itself in a sudden inspiration. At La Libertad the Salvadorean ladies disembarked; a pair of cabins would be vacant. Why should she not move into one of these?

To think was to act. Betty jumped to her feet, went in search of the captain.

She found him in his saloon, writing in a ledger. He greeted her with cautious courtesy, tinged with suspicion. Still he showed no perturbation at the interruption — in fact invited Betty to join him in an aperitif. Betty agreed, and sipped the vermouth to which the captain had added a dash of Campari.

Unable to formulate any euphemism, Betty came directly to the point. "I suppose you know that Isabelle plans to stay aboard, that she's not getting off at La Libertad?"

The captain raised his eyebrows, twirled the glass of vermouth. He seemed uncomfortable. "It is too bad," he said at last. "Too bad for Alan Calder. But I am not surprised."

Betty once more could find no discreet words in which to express herself. "I want to change to another cabin. I'd like to be by myself. When the Salvadorean ladies get off, there'll be two cabins empty. I thought —"

The captain held up his hand, shook his head. "Impossible."

"Impossible?" cried Betty in a voice louder and shriller than she intended. "Why?"

The captain took up a white slip of paper. "This is a radiogram from our agent. From Alan Calder. It is my notification of cargo at La Libertad. We discharge five passengers. Perhaps four, if Mrs. Calder remains on board. We take on five more passengers, to go to Barcelona. There will be eleven passengers, twelve with Mrs. Calder."

Betty wilted in her chair. Tears came to her eyes. "I've got to do something. I can't stand that woman. I won't live in the same cabin with her."

The captain's cordiality was waning. "There is nothing I can do. There are no other accommodations."

"I'll leave the ship myself!" said Betty. "She's impossible! You don't know her! She uses my towel, she doesn't wash her smelly clothes. She loses her shower-cap and takes mine! She's insulting and offensive, she's —" Betty stopped short. "I simply won't stay on the same ship with her!"

"Now, now!" said the captain briskly. "It will be all right."

"Yes," said Betty grimly. "It will be all right. Because I'm going to get off at La Libertad, and catch the next ship through. Alan Calder said I could, and that's what I'm going to do."

The captain cleared his throat, nodded abruptly. "Very well. You must do as you please. The next ship is the *Maggiore*. When we come to La Libertad, you must see Alan Calder. He is the agent. He will make the arrangements; he will tell you if it is possible."

"Possible? Why shouldn't it be possible?"

"There may be no accommodations. We take only twelve passengers. Many people go from El Salvador to Spain. I think it is possible. But you must see Alan Calder."

"Very well," said Betty. "I'll see Alan Calder." She rose to her feet. "Thanks for the vermouth."

Betty went to Cabin #2, a room she hated with all her heart. With luck she would be alone while she freshened herself. But Isabelle was there, preparing for her pre-lunch shower. She wore a white terry-cloth beach robe and wooden clogs; she carried a towel and Betty's bright red shower-cap. Betty spoke in a voice which sounded strange to her own ears: "Damn it, will you leave my things alone?"

Isabelle stared at her. "What are you talking about?"

"My shower-cap."

Isabelle looked at it as if unaware that she had it in her hand. "Oh. It's yours?"

"Yes. It's mine."

"I'm sorry," said Isabelle stiffly. "I just picked it up. I thought it was my own."

"Yours is blue. Mine is red."

Isabelle tossed the cap on the bed, opened her closet, rummaged along the shelf, found her blue shower-cap. Now Betty felt foolish. After all, what was a shower-cap? If someone else had picked it up unthinkingly, as Isabelle apparently had, Betty would have thought nothing about it. But Isabelle!

As Isabelle left the room she looked over her shoulder at Betty. The time was not significant, the occasion of no particular moment. But this was the picture of Isabelle that persisted in Betty's memory: the biscuit-blonde hair, now fluffed and rumpled, with the shower-cap perched on the back of her head like a blue beret; the sweet child's face, the innocence belied by the ice-gray eyes. Then she was gone. She met someone in the hall — Betty heard her voice, then a rumble of laughter: Finsch.

By an odd coincidence, when Betty took her own shower, at her regular time after dinner, she also met Finsch in the corridor. Finsch nodded with his usual half-smiling courtesy, and Betty slipped past, absurdly conscious of his mass and animal magnetism, of her own naked body under the white terry-cloth robe, of the fact that no girl looks her best in her shower-cap.

While she bathed she raged at herself. Jealous! Of Isabelle? Nonsense! Attracted to Finsch? More nonsense! Finsch gave off an aura of sex. He made her aware of herself, aware of him, aware of the processes of reproduction. Otherwise — nothing! Nothing but revulsion.

## 2

The afternoon passed, while the *Garda* drove through blinding sunlight. Five miles to the east volcanoes dappled with forests, farms and meadows lifted into cloudy gloom. Evening came, and night: twelve more hours to La Libertad. The passengers sat on the top deck, excited in their various ways. The Salvadorean ladies twittered like canaries; Alec and Harry Mayberry argued about volcanoes and the interior of the earth. Ora and Betty sat nearby, Ora making plans for the time ashore, Betty saying little. Finsch and Isabelle had pulled a pair of deck-chairs out on the wing of the flying bridge, and sat talking in low tones. Tomorrow would be awkward. The first two men on the ship would be the quarantine officer and Alan Calder. Betty wondered who would tell him and how. There would be a scene. Disgusting, embarrassing. Well, no matter what, she was leaving the ship. She liked Alec and Ora, she tolerated Nello, and she had become rather fond of Harry Mayberry, lecherous old rascal that he was. But there would be people equally likeable on the *Maggiore*, and — she hoped — no one like Finsch or Isabelle.

Someone came to stand behind Betty; a hand reached down, pulled at her ear. "Nello," said Betty, "behave yourself."

"I try very hard," said Nello, "but you are beautiful. I think tonight I will kiss you."

"I think you won't."

A mess-boy came up with bottles of beer on a tray. "Drink up!" called Harry Mayberry. "It's a hot night."

"I accept with pleasure," said Betty. "In fact, I'll order another round myself, right now." And she did so.

The captain came up from the chart-room and accepted a bottle of beer. "Tomorrow at nine o'clock: La Libertad."

"Is there a dock?" Alec asked. "Do we tie up?"

"No, no, no. We anchor. There is no harbor, no breakwater, nothing. The launch will take you to the pier. You will be surprised."

"How so?"

"When you come to the pier, there are big waves. You cannot get off the launch. So you sit in a basket, the crane picks you up. Always the ladies scream."

"After we get ashore, then what?" asked Harry Mayberry. "Beautiful señoritas? Chili con carne? Race tracks? Fiestas?"

The captain laughed. "What is there to do? Nothing. You can drink beer, you can swim on the beach. But you must be careful. Many people die. There are very big waves. Much — what you say? — pullunder."

"Undertow."

"Yes. Undertow."

"What about sharks?" Betty asked.

"There are sharks, but they do not go so close in. You must not swim out past the surf. Then there are sharks. But not so bad here. They are not big, like at Panama. That is where you must never swim, at Panama."

Finsch joined the conversation. "The biggest sharks in the world are in the Sulu Sea. I have killed a white shark thirty-one feet long. In his stomach he carried a piece of iron chain."

Betty turned to the captain. "Why don't we see more sharks? I thought there'd be triangular fins all around us, once we reached the tropics."

The captain shook his head gravely. "They are there. If we should stop the ship, if you should swim in the water, you would see the sharks."

"They are bad creatures," said Finsch in a deep voice, "evil as the devil himself. They know of their own evil, and they hate men because the men know it and kill them."

"Let's talk of the señoritas in La Libertad," said Harry Mayberry. "Do they wear roses over their ears? Do they dance the fandango?"

Finsch chuckled. "They are Indians. There are no señoritas. To see señoritas you must go to San Salvador."

"That's where we're going. La Libertad, San Salvador."

"San Salvador is the city. El Salvador is the country. That is the difference."

Alec asked the captain, "Do we have time to go up to San Salvador?"

"Yes, why not? I will ask the agent. I think we have much coffee to load. We will be one day. So you can go. It is one-half hour by station wagon, through the jungle, up the mountain."

"Fine," said Harry. "If the señoritas don't come to me, I go to them."

Ora laughed jeeringly. "You wouldn't know what to do with a señorita if you found one."

"I know what to do. Whether I could do it or not is another thing."

"One thing I advise you," said the captain, wagging his finger at Ora Cato, "do not get drunk in La Libertad."

"I didn't intend to," said Ora. "Although I must say I didn't intend not to either."

"I will tell you why. When one is drunk he does strange things, especially when it is hot. They will put you in jail and it is hard to get out."

"That is true," said Finsch. "The jail at La Libertad, it is a place one would not care to visit. It is very hot, and very dirty."

Harry Mayberry laughed nervously. "A tourist's paradise. You can drown in the undertow or get thrown into jail."

"No no," said the captain. "It is not as bad as that. But you must not get in any trouble, because you will be very uncomfortable and it will cost you much money. Finsch will know that."

"Yes. It is true. You must bribe everyone, or nothing will be done. I am not sorry to leave El Salvador."

Isabelle spoke in a voice pungent with emotion. "And this is where that damn Alan wanted to maroon me!"

There was an uncomfortable silence. Everyone seemed to know that Isabelle was not planning to debark.

Harry Mayberry cried out suddenly, "Drink up, drink up! Bruno, more beer! This is a pleasure cruise, not a funeral."

# 3

Next morning found the *Garda* only three miles off a beautiful green coast. The beaches foamed with dazzling surf, great mountains sloped back up into the sky, until details were lost in the haze of distance.

At eight o'clock a spatter of buildings could be seen on the shore ahead, and presently a pair of oil-storage tanks. Half an hour later, the dock appeared, a spindly construction protruding a quarter-mile into the ocean, with a rusty red warehouse at the end.

At nine o'clock the *Garda* rounded the cape and coasted into the little bay, at the back of which sat La Libertad.

There was little to see. The town was shrouded in tall trees. Palms lined the beach. On a bluff to the right a long green building with a wide verandah held up a sign HOTEL toward the sea. There were a number of beach-side restaurants, their walls bold with colored signs advertising beer and soft drinks.

The *Garda* drifted to within a half-mile of the shore, then the anchor roared into the water.

Betty was very much on edge. She wanted to catch Alan Calder when he first came aboard, before he went looking for Isabelle. Then she could ask her question, get a quick answer. She hoped, but feared it would be impossible.

Isabelle stood with Finsch on the wing of the flying bridge, her fingers twisting together. Finsch wore his broad-brimmed hat, and seemed unperturbed. Nello came up beside Betty, put his arm around her waist, bent his handsome head over her. "Nello!" said Betty crossly. "There's a time and place for everything. This is definitely not it!"

"Tell me when!"

"Never!"

"Never? A very long time!"

"I know."

Harry Mayberry joined them, to Nello's disgruntlement.

"Curtain about to go up on Act Two," said Harry. "Look at 'em. Who tells the husband?"

"Who generally does, in this kind of situation?" Betty asked.

"There's no rule," said Harry. "I've had it worked on me all kinds of ways. My first wife disappeared with the bank-roll. My second wife rode off behind a jockey. She said she was going to divorce me, but I never heard. My third wife —"

"How could you marry if you weren't sure whether your second wife had divorced you?"

"My second wife? Hell, I don't even know about my first wife. I just marry 'em."

"Harry Mayberry! You're a bigamist!"

"Maybe so. Nobody ever lost any sleep over it."

Nello pointed. "There comes the launch."

They squinted, trying to pick out faces and shapes among the men who stood on the deck.

"This is uncomfortable," said Betty gritting her teeth. "I'd like to be somewhere else."

"So would Isabelle," said Harry Mayberry. "She's turning all colors of the rainbow."

"That's the difficulty. She can't be somewhere else."

"And here comes Alan, happy as a lark, eager to carry wifey across the threshold of the new thatch hut."

The launch came plunging over the blue swells — nearer and nearer. A man in light brown slacks and a short-sleeved white shirt, still face-less, waved an arm toward the ship. That would be Alan. Betty turned away from the rail. It was like watching an execution. She had her own business to attend to. If she could only take Alan aside for fifteen sec-onds! She need ask only one question: "Mr. Calder — can I stop over a month and continue on the *Maggiore*?" He could say yes or no — it would be as simple as that.

"Excuse me," said Betty. She ran down to the main deck, to where the deck-hands had lowered the embarkation ladder.

The launch came lunging and plunging across the swells. On the deck stood two men in uniform, wearing guns; a man with a briefcase, in dark glasses and a brick-colored suit; a man in white, with a pasty flat face and a thin red beard; and Alan Calder. Alan sought along the ship for sight of Isabelle, who had moved somewhere out of sight. Alan's posture was strained with eagerness and impatience.

Betty waited tensely at the top of the ladder. The captain came to stand beside her. "Aha! I see you are anxious."

"I want to see him before he hears the bad news."

"Wise, wise. Alan Calder, he is an excited man." The captain, affable now that Betty was leaving the ship, patted her on the shoulder. "You come with me to my cabin. That's where we will go, and you may settle your business. I think I will say a little word to him. It is unpleasant, but the captain must do many unpleasant things."

The launch drew close to the side of the ship, rising and falling on the swells. At last Isabelle showed herself; Alan waved his arm vigorously. Isabelle's greeting apparently was not effusive, because Alan's arm became a trifle limp.

The launch gingerly eased close to the embarkation ladder. The man in dark glasses and brick-colored suit waited his opportunity, jumped across. A deck-hand caught and steadied him. Alan Calder followed, then the man with the red beard.

The captain waited at the top of the gangway, shook hands first with the man in the dark glasses, then Alan Calder. "We go to my cabin," said the captain to Alan. "The chief mate takes care of the doctor and the harbor-master." He spoke in Spanish to the man in dark glasses, who bowed punctiliously, pushed through the Salvadorean ladies toward the mess-hall, followed by the man in the red beard.

Alan tried to move away. "Just one minute. I'll run up, say hello to my wife, then I'll be right with you."

The captain caught his arm. "First with me! Then you see your wife. There is plenty time. She cannot leave the ship. One moment only."

Calder acceded with the poorest possible grace, growling under his breath.

"To my cabin, then," said the captain, signaling Betty to follow.

They climbed to the bridge deck; the captain ushered them into his cabin with rather more ceremony than necessary. "Be seated. A glass of cognac?"

Alan nodded dourly; Betty refused.

The captain opened his locker, brought out two glasses and a bottle. This was Betty's opportunity.

"Mr. Calder, in Los Angeles you told me I could wait over in El Salvador, and catch the next ship — the *Maggiore*. Is that still possible?"

Alan drummed his fingers on the table. "I suppose so. I'm not certain. I'll have to check at the office."

"When can I find out for sure?"

"As soon as I go ashore — in an hour or so. I won't know till then. Meet me at my office."

"Where is your office?"

"I've moved; I'm up in the Miramar. Anybody will show you: the big green hotel up on the hill... Now, Captain —"

Captain Frascatore held up his hand. "Be calm, Alan. I must talk to you a moment."

Betty said, "Excuse me," and started to rise to her feet. But in the doorway stood Isabelle, and behind, looking indifferent, was Finsch.

Alan jumped to his feet, ran forward, colliding with Betty, pushing her back into her chair. "Isabelle darling! You're here! Hurray!" He held out his arms.

Isabelle's expression was bleak. She swayed out of reach. Alan stopped short, blinking, staring back and forth between Isabelle and Finsch.

"Alan," said Isabelle, "could you step out on deck? I've got something to say to you."

Alan moved forward a slow step or two. Betty caught a glimpse of his face. He knew what was going to happen. Betty huddled in the chair, feeling miserable and cold.

"What's the trouble?" faltered Alan.

Isabelle could wait no longer; it was pent up inside her and had to come out. Her voice came from the corridor, low and harsh with an ugly glottal rasp. "I'll make it short and sweet. I'm not getting off here. I'm going on to Europe."

"Oh, you are?"

"Yes. I am."

"What have I done?" Alan's voice rose into something like a whine. "Why do you treat me like this?"

"Let's not go into details, Alan."

"After all, isn't this rather sudden? Haven't you considered me at all?"

"No, not at all. I'm thinking of me. If I don't, nobody else will."

"I've always thought of you! I've put you first, last and always!"

"There's no use talking about it. I'm sorry, but that's it, and that's all I'm going to say. Except that I'll get a divorce somewhere, as soon as I can."

Alan could not contain himself. He burst out, half-stuttering, "This is a fine howdy-do! I suppose you expect me to roll over and play dead." He suddenly took notice of Finsch. "I catch on now. My good friend Mik Finsch. He's at the bottom of this." Alan laughed, an unnatural sardonic bark. "You don't know much about Finsch, do you?"

"I know enough."

"Oh. You admit it?"

"Let's not have a production, Alan. Lots of people decide they don't want to live together any more. I'm one of them."

"You're picking Mik Finsch to live with, hey? Sister, you've picked a bad hombre."

Finsch pursed his lips, made a gesture with the palm of his hand, as if to imply that Alan was over-excited and must not be taken seriously.

Alan took a quick step forward. Isabelle jerked back. "Keep away from me."

"Did he tell you why he's leaving El Salvador? No? Well, I'll put you wise. The cops told him to leave. He's lucky. He nearly killed a girl. Her parents took six hundred dollars instead of prosecuting. I imagine Finsch had to square a few cops too."

Finsch made a thoughtful rumbling in his throat.

Alan's voice mounted. "But I don't care, Finsch. Take her. She's yours. There's only one little detail. You'll have to pay for her. She cost me three thousand dollars."

"That's enough out of you, Alan!" Isabelle said viciously.

"Shut up! I'm talking to Finsch. Cash, hard, cold cash. I paid for her, you get her after you've paid me."

"What are you talking about?" said Finsch.

"Talking about? I told you. I've got a valuable piece of merchandise here. I bought it, I paid for it. I'm not going to give it away."

"You are like a crazy man."

"Not at all. I'll show you. A picture is worth a thousand words. Come in here where there's light. Everybody can see." Alan backed into the room. "Come, Finsch. You're buying, you might as well see what you're getting."

Finsch sauntered into the cabin. He nodded to the captain, ignored Betty. Isabelle stayed in the corridor, quivering with hate.

Laughing with great gaiety, Alan took a photograph from his wallet. "That's us, a week before we were married. Alan and Isabelle. Nice young couple."

Finsch picked up the photograph, looked at it with detached curiosity. He raised his eyebrows, tossed it back on the table. Betty had a quick glimpse: a stalwart Alan, unsmiling and business-like; a young woman who was Isabelle and yet not Isabelle. The woman in the photograph was thin; skin stretched over her face like parchment on a lamp. Her chest was a birdcage, her legs were like poles. The face was only vaguely Isabelle. The mouth was curved in a shy grin, the nose was extraordinary. It hung down from her forehead like a stalactite.

"Remarkable, isn't it?" said Alan. "Isabelle was a good sport in those days. She had courage. See what a nice smile she had? I married her for that smile. She began to put on weight after we were married. Her complexion cleared up. She began to take trouble with her hair. I took a look at her one day. I said, 'Isabelle, let's go to a specialist and have your nose straightened.' She cried, 'Don't you love me the way I am?' Anyway we went. Three thousand bucks. But what a change. Not only in looks. I knew she was gone the first day she came home. She couldn't keep away from the mirror. Well, Finsch, that's the story. She cost me three thousand. You can have her — for three thousand."

Finsch smiled, took a cigar from his pocket, bit the end off, and still smiling, lit the cigar. "Your wife is a free agent, eh?"

"I certainly am," said Isabelle. "I'm not going to stay in this stinking hole, and that's flat."

"How are you going to leave?" asked Alan, mildly curious.

"Leave? The same way I came. I'm not stirring from this ship."

"Ah, but you'll have to. You only took passage to La Libertad."

"So what? I'll buy the rest of the trip right now."

"From who?"

"From the captain."

"Go ahead."

Isabelle turned to the captain. "How much does it cost to Europe?"

The captain held out his hands. "I can't help you. Alan is the agent. Maybe he already has sold out the passages. We are only allowed to take twelve passengers."

"That's just silly. I've got the cabin, and I'm going to stay in it."

Finsch blew a thoughtful plume of smoke into the air. He looked from the corner of his eye at Alan. "May I ask, are there any passages available?"

"As of this moment, no."

"Are you trying blackmail?" Finsch's voice was soft and dull.

"I'll tell you once again, Finsch. You wouldn't have looked at her before I blew the three grand. I don't propose to spend that money for your benefit. You pay me what she cost, and she'll get passage on the *Garda*. Otherwise — no."

"Foolishness," said Finsch in a voice of absolute boredom.

"Not to me," said Alan. "In a way I'm glad it's over — because I've known it was going to happen. You two deserve each other."

"Thank you," said Finsch.

"Well, how about it, Finsch? Is she worth three thousand?"

Isabelle turned to Finsch, started to speak, held her tongue. Finsch rolled his eyes toward the ceiling.

"Make an offer, Finsch. Give me whatever you think she's worth!"

Isabelle turned and ran down the corridor. Finsch backed out of the cabin, went placidly after her.

A steward came into the cabin, spoke to the captain. The captain nodded, rose heavily to his feet. "The doctor and the harbor-master, they wait for me."

"How long before we can go ashore?" asked Betty.

"Perhaps in half an hour. Very soon. When the launch comes back."

# Chapter VII

## 1

Betty climbed to the top deck, went out on the flying bridge, but the sun blazed with such white passion that she retreated under the awning. The air was heavy and quiet, for the wind had died with the ship's motion; every object within vision glittered and trembled with heat. Betty's blouse became limp, her jeans clung to her legs like wet paper. She looked longingly toward the town, where there was at least the illusion of coolness under the great green trees.

A tug pulled away from the pier, and started toward the *Garda*, towing a lighter piled high with large tawny sacks, evidently coffee. Betty searched for the launch, which was nowhere to be seen. Behind the pier, perhaps? Then from alongside came a thrum and sputter, and the launch slanted away through the sparkling green waves. Betty ran to the rail, fearing that she had missed connections. But the launch carried only one man: Alan Calder. Evidently the launch would take him ashore, then return.

Betty returned to her seat under the awning, considering the immediate future. Alan had as good as assured her that she could transfer to the *Maggiore*. Conditions had changed, of course: Alan might refuse to provide Isabelle passage on the *Garda*. If this were the case, Betty would have Cabin #2 to herself... She toyed with the possibilities of the situation. If Isabelle disembarked, then Betty would be inclined to stay aboard. Finsch was revolting, but could be avoided. Nevertheless it seemed probable that Alan, however reluctantly, would arrange passage for Isabelle. After all, this was his job, and he had no right to discriminate for purely personal reasons.

Alec and Ora appeared dressed for shore, and joined her under the awning. "We've got till midnight tonight," said Ora. "We're going up to San Salvador; are you coming?"

"No. At least not right away."

Ora looked at her sidewise. "You may not get another chance."

"I'll come along later...I have some business with Alan Calder."

"Is he in a state to do business? There was a terrible row, so we hear."

"I was right in the middle of it." Betty described the unpleasant quarter-hour. "Alan may be upset, but at least he knows the worst."

"He put Finsch very nicely on the spot," said Alec. "Finsch doesn't like to spend his money. I've seen Isabelle signing bar checks."

"There he goes now," said Ora. The tug which had brought out the lighter was returning to the dock. On the forward deck stood Finsch, in his gray suit and broad-brimmed hat. "And here comes the launch. We can go ashore now."

Betty looked down at her clothes — blue jeans, blouse, sandals. "I wonder — do you think these clothes are all right?"

"They look all right to me," said Alec. "Why shouldn't they be?"

"I've heard that some of these countries are peculiar about clothes. I don't want to get thrown in jail for indecency. Especially after what I hear of the jails."

"Indecency is in the mind of the beholder," Alec told her.

"As well as in the tightness of the britches," said Ora.

"There's the launch," said Betty. "We'd better go below."

Betty went to her cabin, changed her limp blouse for a fresh white polo shirt, took a little white purse, ran down to the main deck.

The passengers stood waiting in a line by the gangway: the Salvadorean ladies with their luggage, Nello, Harry Mayberry, Ora and Alec.

The launch swung in a circle, nosed through the sunlit green water close up under the ship. The Salvadorean ladies started down the ladder. At the bottom a deck-hand steadied each in turn, then at the exact instant, when the deck of the launch rose to the level of the platform, thrust her across to a man on the launch.

Betty had not appreciated the size of the swells until she herself stood at the bottom of the ladder. One instant the launch dropped far below, the next it lofted up on a great green slope, then down, then up, then — *"Ahora!"* And Betty found herself on the pitching deck of the launch, groping for a hand-hold.

Ora followed, then Alec and Nello and Harry, and finally three of the ship's officers. The launch sheered away, the *Garda* fell astern. Isabelle had not come — no surprise, thought Betty. She must detest everything Salvadorean! Also she might be wary of leaving the ship for fear of difficulty in returning. Finsch presumably had gone for his personal belongings, or possibly to dicker with Alan.

Betty looked back over the counter of the launch to the *Garda*. It sat low in the water: black hull, white deck-house, red and green funnel. Ugly, slow, hot, trustworthy, nice old ship, thought Betty. But not three more weeks with Isabelle. I'd be ready for murder myself... Hm. Strange that word should pop into her mind. Anyway — no more *Garda*. Alan had made his gesture; now he'd allow Isabelle to go to hell in her own way. He had no real reason to put her ashore. Still — why not? Isabelle had hurt him intensely. Alan was an obstinate man... Betty threw up her hands. I can't figure it out. I'll get off the *Garda*, spend a month in Central America. Aboard the *Maggiore* there'll be a new set of faces, a new group of personalities. And so to Europe.

Nello clambered across the deck, settled beside her. "Are you enjoying yourself?"

"Oh yes. It's nice to get off the ship."

"Sit just so," said Nello. "I will take your picture, with the ship in the background." He opened his camera, adjusted time and aperture, focused, shot the picture. "Excellent!" He seated himself once more. "I have a good idea. When we get to San Salvador, you and I, we will lose the others, go off by ourselves. What do you think?"

Betty shook her head. "You're too late, Nello. I've already made plans with the others to lose you."

Nello sat stiffly upright.

"Don't be irritated, Nello," said Betty laughing. "I'm not going to San Salvador."

"You are not? Why?"

"I have business in La Libertad."

Nello was amused. "What kind of business is this?"

In spite of Betty's resolve to say nothing until her plans were definite, it all came out. "I may leave the ship and stop over in Central America a month."

"What is this?" cried Nello dramatically. He beckoned to Alec and Ora and Harry. "Do you hear this? Betty is leaving us!"

"We rather suspected as much," said Alec.

"I'm not sure yet, that's why I haven't said anything. I won't really know until after I've seen Alan Calder."

There were polite regrets and protests which Betty dealt with expeditiously. "You're not rid of me yet. There may not be space on the *Maggiore*."

Ora said thoughtfully, "Alan may not want to let you off the *Garda*."

"Why on earth not?"

"Because then there'd be space aboard ship for Isabelle."

Betty snorted. "He'd better not dare think of such a thing!"

The launch approached the pier, no more than a warehouse perched on piles, connected by a trestle to the shore. The launch edged in under the warehouse, and after some alarming maneuvers beside the piles, with the green swells hissing and sucking past, made fast to a trailing loop of rope. From above came the sound of machinery, the screech of metal wheels. A boom swung out from the warehouse, dangling a large box. Down came the box, swinging and twisting; the launch lofted up on a swell; the two met with a thud.

Before they had time to protest, the four Salvadorean ladies were bundled into the box. They seated themselves at either end, clutching the rope slings for dear life. The crane heaved, the launch fell out from under, the box swung up into the air, and into the warehouse.

Seconds later it returned for a second load: Betty, Alec, Ora and Harry Mayberry. Swoop, lurch, spin — out of the sun, into the shadow, thump to the floor of the warehouse.

Nello came up in the next load, along with the three ship's officers; everyone set out for shore. The time was eleven-thirty. The sun pressed a white-hot thumb upon the heads of the travelers, the water glittered and glared beneath them. Harry Mayberry lamented the evil destiny which brought him to the tropics. Nello, with sweat streaming down his own face, assured him that La Libertad was cool, even refreshing, compared to the Red Sea.

They approached the end of the pier, crossed a beach of round gray rocks the size of baseballs, clattering and grinding in the surf. A pair of stocky dark-skinned soldiers in khaki uniforms, with flat faces and eyes like coffee beans, stepped forward.

"*Donde van ustedes?*"

"*Somos turistas,*" said Alec in careful Spanish. "*Vamos a San Salvador; esta noche volveremos a la barca.*"

The soldier pointed to the zipper bag which Alec carried. "*Que tiene? Vamos a ver.*"

Alec opened the bag, the soldier peered inside. "*Bueno.*" He waved them past with lordly condescension.

They paused to mop at their sweat under the trees which lined the esplanade. "Here's where we separate," said Betty. "I turn off down the beach."

"Oh come along to the plaza," Harry Mayberry urged her. "I'm buying the beer."

Betty allowed herself to be persuaded, and they all set out for the plaza, up a cobbled street lined with ocher-yellow, white and pale-blue shops.

"I smell something," said Ora. "I believe it is that dead dog in the street."

Behind came the sound of tires, a mellow blast of horn. A cream-colored Cadillac swept past, driven by a moon-faced man in purple sun-glasses. The car bumped across the dog, and proceeded.

"I'd like to throw it into the car beside him," said Ora.

"Don't," said Harry. "He's the Chief of Police."

"How do you know?"

"They have a certain look."

"Let's get out of here."

They walked up the street to the plaza. Vendors swarmed the sidewalks; children crawled in the dirt, putting things in their mouths: sticks, cigarette butts, dog manure. What they had no taste for they spat out. There were dozens of smells: hot vegetation, frying meat, sewer gas, brilliantine, stale beer, carrion, dust.

Harry Mayberry bought ice-cold beer from a booth; Nello took pictures of his shipmates, of the plaza, of Betty drinking from her bottle of beer. Across the street a line of station wagons marked *San Salvador — La Libertad* waited for passengers; there was also an old blue bus. Alec went off to make arrangements; Betty took her leave of the group. "Goodbye, have a good time, and don't forget: the ship sails at midnight!"

# 2

Betty returned to the esplanade, proceeded south beside the beach. Surf crashed and thundered over the rocks; trees swayed and dipped above her, leaves glowing in the sunlight.

The esplanade presently twisted inland, became a rutted road leading through trees, vines, creepers and plants, past huts built of sticks and thatch. Pigs browsed in the refuse, big-eyed children watched as she walked by.

After another fifty yards the road curved down to the bathing beach, then ended at a flight of ancient stone steps leading up the hill. Betty started up the steps. A red-eyed old man in a tattered sombrero, sitting on the lowest step, held out his hand, mumbling plaintively. Drunk, thought Betty. She opened her purse, found a dime, dropped it into his hand. It fell between his fingers. While he searched with heavy-lidded eyes, Betty hastened past him up the stairs.

She saw the hotel ahead, half-hidden under trees. The road, flanked by low palms and broad-leafed bushes, continued past and around the hill, with a wide well-kept path angling off under the trees toward the hotel. As she entered the path Betty saw a signpost reading: HOTEL MIRAMAR, and two smaller signs; the first reading *Juan Ortiz y Escandell, Abogado,* the second *Alan J. Calder, General Shipping Agent.*

Betty followed the path through banana plants, banks of bougainvillea and hibiscus, a thicket of bamboo and out upon a terrace along the front of the hotel.

A waiter looked up from laying tables — a handsome lad sleek as a cat, with smooth coffee-and-milk skin, long straight hair glistening with oil. He bowed and clicked his heels extravagantly. *"A sus ordenes, señorita!"*

Betty smiled politely, hoping he spoke English. "I want to speak to Mr. Calder."

The waiter bowed once more. "I go see."

He walked across the terrace, around the corner of the hotel. Betty sauntered after him, stopping to admire the view of ocean, beach, esplanade, and town. A quarter-mile off-shore the *Garda* swung at anchor.

The waiter returned. "Somebody is with Mr. Calder, I hear the voices. In a few minutes, maybe you can see him. You like something to drink?"

"What do you have?"

"You say, we got her."

"I say — orange soda!"

"We got."

He brought the soda, and also, because Betty was young and pretty, a small dish of shrimp. "Nice view here, you think so?"

"I think so. Very nice view."

"You like La Libertad?"

Betty hesitated. "The esplanade is very nice." She opened her purse. "How much is this?"

"Is twenty centavos."

"Can I pay you in American money?"

"Sure!"

"Here's twenty-five cents," said Betty. "That should be enough."

The waiter seemed in no hurry to leave. He pointed to the *Garda*. "You go away on the ship?"

Not if she could help it. "No. I go to San Salvador."

"I go somewhere pretty soon. La Libertad, it is square. You know what square means?"

"Oh yes."

"I am not square. I play guitar, I sing, I dance. You like to see me dance?"

"As long as it's free."

"I show you. I like to dance with pretty girls."

"Oh, I'm not dancing. Just you."

The waiter nodded agreeably. "I dance the tap dance. In Mexico I make much money. Maybe Buenos Aires. I show you." He held his hands over his head. "La la la-la, la la-la."

"Enrique!" A woman's voice, shrill and angry, came from the hotel.

Enrique the waiter dropped his arms. He drew his dignity about him, bowed to Betty. "Mr. Calder he come pretty soon."

Enrique went into the restaurant. A burst of angry chatter diminished as a door slammed.

There was silence on the terrace, with nothing to be heard but the faint hum of insects, the rumble and sigh of the surf, the rustle of leaves and the far call of a bird. It was easy to understand why Alan preferred the Hotel Miramar to a more central location.

She finished her orange soda, went to the edge of the terrace, where she picked two or three flowers. They were red as geraniums and smelled of honey. Wishing Alan would hurry, she strolled across the terrace to the far end of the hotel. The ground fell abruptly away into the sea, a hundred feet below. A railed-in walkway ran beside the hotel, past a door where another of Alan's signs hung, then up a slope overgrown with shrubbery and into the road above.

Standing at the corner of the hotel Betty heard voices, indistinct through the sound of the sea, which seemed to come from one of Alan's windows. The louder and more emphatic seemed to be Alan's...Yes, definitely it was Alan. He seemed to come close to the window, for his voice was louder. "Certainly, why not? I'll give you the receipt — at the bank, because that's where we're going. As soon as that check gets credited to my account, you get what you want."

Betty sighed, tapped her fingers on the rail. Hurry up, Alan; it's dull standing here.

Alan moved away from the window; the voices were muffled again.

There was a period of silence: half a minute. Then there was a sharp report, an explosion. Betty jumped around, stared wide-eyed at the window.

She started forward, then halted, watching the door fascinated. Presently it would open, someone would step forth. He would see her, his eyes would stare at her.

A black object sailed from the window, spinning out into the air. Betty's eyes followed it. A black object with a white handle. It curved down toward the water, but the slope of the cliff was deceiving; instead of landing in the water, the object struck a jut of rock, clattered off at an angle, slid into a crevice.

Betty's feet were heavy as stones. She must run. In a minute it would be too late. Already it was too late. The door opened, slow and stealthy. Betty backed slowly away, off the walkway. She stumbled, staggered back, turned, ran.

Enrique had come out of the restaurant and was watching her. Betty slowed her pace to a fast walk. *"Ay, señorita!"* called Enrique. *"Que pasa?* There was the noise of a gun, no?"

"I do not know," said Betty. "I do not want to know."

Enrique shrugged in bafflement. He scratched his jaw, pursed his lips, shrugged again, evidently not caring to know too much either.

Betty quickened her pace, left the terrace almost at a trot. She wanted to look over her shoulder to see if someone stood at the corner of the hotel watching her. But she did not dare...She stopped short, suddenly angry and indignant. She was Betty Haverhill of Menlo Park, California, who took orders from no one. Defiantly she swung around. The terrace was empty, except for Enrique, who looked after her with perplexity.

This isn't so good, thought Betty. A shot. Enrique sees me running across the terrace. Suppose someone is hurt, what will he tell the police? Betty had a vision of the police station, dirty and hot, with peeling yellow walls. She envisioned the officials, bleak dark men in mustard-colored uniforms, calling at her in Spanish, bellowing when she could not reply. The *Garda* sailed at midnight. Alan could not help her now.

She walked rapidly back the way she had come, her stomach stiff with apprehension. She came out on the esplanade. There was the *Garda*, snug and secure. Once aboard she'd be safe; they couldn't take her off...Or could they? Ridiculous, she thought; I've done nothing, I have nothing whatever to fear...She saw a policeman ahead, busy with official duties. An old man sat on one of the benches — the same beggar who had accosted Betty on the steps. He was looking up at the policeman, shaking his head blearily. The policeman raised his booted leg, toppled the old man off the bench. The old man lay in a heap mumbling curses. The policeman watched him intently a moment, then strolled up the esplanade. Betty walked past rapidly, her heart beating. She could not get aboard the *Garda* fast enough.

She half-ran down the trestle, out into the blaze of heat, out over the beach with its crashing surf and roaring stones. She was hungry, weary, nervous. Once aboard the *Garda* she could rest and think. The police might come aboard, then she could tell what she knew. It was nothing, really — only where the gun lay hidden. Possibly the police would not come out. They might arrest someone else.

She neared the warehouse. No shouts behind her, no running policemen. She entered the great dim cave, rejoicing in the coolness. Dodging the traveling cranes she went to one of the loading areas, looked down along the line of piles. The water, opaque in the sunlight, became luminous aquarium-green in the shade. Two lighters wallowed in the swells, receiving coffee. The launch was nowhere to be seen. It might be on the far side of the *Garda*.

Betty went to a man in bright blue slacks and a white basket-weave shirt. He carried a clipboard, a ball-point pencil, and seemed to be in authority. "When can I go back to the ship?" she asked.

"Launch come pretty soon. One-half hour."

"Thank you." Betty sank limply upon a convenient sack of coffee. Her legs ached from the fast walking, she felt bedraggled and dank. Her mind was a maze, full of simultaneous emotions. It was an effort to think. Her apprehension was of course foolish; the police would know she had nothing to do with the situation. But they would ask, why did you run? Why did you not report this occurrence? She had panicked: this was the painful truth.

Betty tormented herself with pictures of Alan wounded, bleeding to death, while she fled — but the pictures carried no conviction. There had been finality to the shot.

Now there was nothing to prevent Isabelle from continuing to Europe aboard the *Garda*. Between Isabelle and the Salvadorean police, Isabelle seemed the lesser evil. Of course, Finsch... She saw Finsch. Sedately he strolled the length of the warehouse, fanning himself with his broad-brimmed hat. Betty watched him with dilated eyes; her legs tense beneath her.

Finsch apparently did not see her. He went to the checker, greeted him as an acquaintance. The checker responded with no great friendliness. Betty could barely hear their voices over the swash of waves through the pilings; they seemed to be talking Spanish. Finsch turned, gestured toward the shore, shook his head in humorous disapproval. The checker bowed formally, and turned away. Finsch came toward Betty, seated himself on a sack. "Now you have seen La Libertad. What do you think of the place?"

"I don't care for it."

"It is not attractive. I, of course, lived eighteen kilometers to the north, at Finca San Sebastian. My luggage comes aboard the ship today. I have made the arrangements." He fanned himself with his hat. "It is very hot, eh? A heat like fly-paper. No place for a woman. Alan Calder made a great mistake."

Betty's voice seemed to speak of itself, in a strained and high-pitched tone. "I suppose you've come to an understanding?"

"I?" Finsch seemed surprised. "It is not for me to interfere."

"I thought you went ashore to see him."

"No. I went to care for my luggage. I have one or two precious things. It is not for me to see Alan Calder. His wife does not love him. That is no reason to be a crazy man, eh?"

Betty said nothing. Finsch raised his eyebrows, said no more. Ten minutes passed. Betty sat quiet and painfully tense, knees pressed together, arms close to her sides. There was the sound of a motor; Betty jumped to her feet. It was the launch, bringing half a dozen of the ship's crew to shore. The checker waved to the crane; it rolled forward, picked up the wooden box. The checker signaled to Betty. "Señorita."

Betty gingerly stepped into the box, seated herself. Finsch settled at the opposite end. Their knees almost touched. Betty's flesh crawled. This man had once kissed her! Their eyes met for an instant. Betty looked swiftly away.

The basket swung up, out, and down, thudded on the deck of the launch. Finsch jumped heavily out, offered his hand to Betty, which she ignored.

The launch cast off and roared back out to sea. The time was now about two o'clock. The sun glittered from the water, drops of warm spray blew into Betty's face. She sat on one side of the hatch, Finsch stood beside the wheel-house. She looked back toward the shore. There was the esplanade, the bright green trees, the gray beach, the glimpses of sun-struck paint. And up on the hill, the hotel, placid and peaceful. The situation was unbelievable, a ghastly hallucination. The heat? She glanced surreptitiously toward Finsch. He stood trying to light a cigar, cupping his hands into the wind. He looked so easy, so careless... Betty turned another desperate look toward shore. Had she made a fool of herself?

No, she thought after a moment. Of course not. If someone had come from Alan's office to find her staring, it would have meant real danger. To have flown to the police would have caused real nuisance, if not worse... But what of justice? Betty felt a pang of conscience. She would talk to the captain, she would tell him everything: after all, it was his responsibility, not hers.

The launch moved in under the embarkation ladder. The seaman on gangway watch came down to catch her as she jumped across... She ran quickly up the steps.

# Chapter VIII

## 1

THE PURSER, A SALLOW SLIGHT young man, leaned over the rail. Betty asked, "Where is Captain Frascatore?"

The purser waved his hand limply toward shore. "He go to have lunch with the agent. He come back after a while."

Betty went aimlessly to the mess-hall, which was dark, with curtains drawn across the portholes, and relatively cool. She sat down a moment, then restlessly jumped to her feet. Leaving the mess-hall, she walked aft past the galley, where the cooks peeled vegetables for dinner.

She climbed the stairs to Cabin #2, sat on her bunk, discouraged and apprehensive. How had she managed to get in such a mess? Thousands of people took passage on ships without involving themselves in trouble. It was inevitable that the police would come out for her; they would take her ashore, the *Garda* would sail. With no one else on hand to accuse, who knew what might happen?

Fingers clutched together, she sat staring at imaginary pictures: the Salvadorean jail and its presumably unpleasant sanitary facilities; the moon-faced man in the Cadillac standing spraddle-legged over her, bullying and smirking... She laughed weakly. What foolishness this was! Why did she work so hard to frighten herself? The captain would never allow her to be taken from the ship; he was responsible for her safety! If necessary she would lock herself in her cabin and refuse to come out till the ship sailed. She had put up with Isabelle thus far, she could manage the rest of the trip... Somehow.

The cabin was suffocatingly hot, sweat was running into her eyes. She went to the porthole, looked out, but could see nothing of the town. She stood indecisively in the middle of the room, thinking about the shower, the jets of cool water. It meant leaving the cabin — oh well, if they wanted her bad enough to come out to the ship, presumably they'd break open a door. Locking herself in would only make matters worse. After all, she had done nothing, except run back to the ship when she should have notified the police. She was actually guiltless. She had nothing to worry about. A shower, definitely! For a wonder her towel was fresh and unsullied; for a wonder her shower-cap was where she had left it.

The cool water left her refreshed, revitalized. She put on her white shorts and a fresh white halter, and went up to the top deck. Finsch and Isabelle sat under the awning talking earnestly. They ignored Betty; she said nothing to them, but dragged a chair to the other side of the deck, and settled herself.

Isabelle sat in sulky silence, but Finsch seemed almost jocund. Nor had he shown any trace of strain returning on the launch. Betty moved uneasily in her chair. Had her senses deceived her? Surely a white-handled object had come spinning out of Alan's window!

She tried to remember the exact look of Finsch's gun. After all, there were many guns with white butts; the two need not necessarily be the same. If she wanted to make sure she could go back to La Libertad, scramble down the cliff and recover the gun. That was the one way of making sure. The prospect of returning to shore was not at all attractive! Still, it would be a relief to know instead of merely suspecting… Another way suggested itself. It was rather ticklish — so ticklish in fact that shivers ran up her back. She looked across the deck. Finsch was leaning back in his chair, eyes half-closed, the very picture of a retired planter taking his ease. Betty jumped to her feet. It would be no more than the work of a minute.

Her heart beating rapidly, she descended the ladder, walked swiftly to Finsch's cabin. She stopped, listened a few seconds, tried the door. It was unlocked. She entered, hooked the door open, drew the curtain across the gap: at least she could hear if anyone approached. She reached under the bed, pulled out the big leather suitcase, lifted it to the bed, swung back the lid.

Underwear, shirts, handkerchiefs, folded with exactitude. A slim packet of letters and documents, bound with a rubber band. The orb of jade. The *kris*. The black plastic cylinder of gas. But no ivory-handled automatic pistol — unless... Betty felt under the stacked underwear, a process which raised the whole pile, tilted it forward. The jade ball rolled forward, out on the bed. Betty made a frantic grab, contriving only to send the ball flying. It struck the deck with an unpleasant sound, splitting into two almost equal pieces.

"Oh lord," whispered Betty, picking up the pieces, "what have I done?"

She hurriedly smoothed out the clothes, piled them as before, then took up the bits of jade, pushed them together. When she relaxed the pressure, they fell apart. If she cemented them, Finsch might never notice... But time, time, time! She heard footsteps and froze, going hot and cold. The footsteps turned down the thwart-ship corridor and out of hearing. Betty hurriedly closed the suitcase, slid it under the bed. She took the two pieces of jade, slid the curtain back, stepped into the corridor, closed the door.

Her heart was pumping with unpleasant force and rapidity. She had only been in the cabin three or four minutes, but what if Finsch had caught her? Especially in view of the fact that the gun was gone.

She went to the stairs, climbed as nonchalantly as possible to the top deck. Finsch and Isabelle sat as before. Two hemispheres of jade. A drop of cement — a sphere again — Finsch none the wiser. Betty returned to her cabin, rummaged through her suitcases. Where was that darn cement? Here — in the side pocket. With trembling fingers, she squeezed a few drops upon the fractured surfaces, rubbed them smooth with her finger, clapped the two halves together. Little bubbles of cement oozed out along the crack; she wiped them off with her thumb. Five minutes should be enough — even less.

Holding the ball tightly pressed together, she looked out of the porthole. At least her fear of the police had diminished. Finsch's gun was gone from his suitcase, she knew where it could be found. That should be enough to satisfy them.

The ball seemed stuck together. To a casual glance it appeared sound and whole.

She left the cabin, climbed half-way up the ladder, listened. Had she looked, she would have seen Finsch standing, stretching his arms. But Betty only listened. The voices were low and even. Time to duck into the cabin, to drop the ball into the suitcase, and be away, thought Betty, with no one ever the wiser.

She swung back down the stairs, ran along the corridor to Finsch's cabin. She entered, closed the door behind her; she would only be an instant. She slid the suitcase out, opened it, dropped the jade ball in, closed it. And now she heard Finsch's footsteps, directly outside the door, his hand almost to the knob. In terror she thrust herself underneath the bed, wriggling behind the suitcase, dragging her legs under and out of sight even as the door swung open.

Finsch came into the room, closed the door. Hissing tunelessly between his teeth, he came forward, tossed his hat upon the writing desk.

Looking over the top of the suitcase, Betty watched Finsch's legs. They walked to the closet. The closet door opened, closed, the legs returned. In front of the bed they became stock-still. The hissing ceased. Betty began to sweat the acrid cold sweat of fear. His suspicions somehow had been aroused, he was on the point of bending to peer under the bed... But Finsch was undressing. He sat on the bed with a soft grunt of relaxation, reached down, unlaced his shoes, removed them, pulled off his socks. The heavy feet stood planted two feet in front of Betty's face. One leg rose in the air, a loose pant-leg dangled, then the other, and Finsch was trouserless. His shorts dropped around his ankles, he kicked them loose. Betty thought with sudden hope, he's off to take a shower!

Finsch took his dressing gown from the closet, wrapped it around himself. He thrust his feet into clogs, took his towel and soap. Betty lay itching with impatience. Go, go, go! Let me out of here! I'll never do anything like this again!

But Finsch came back, clattering across the floor in his clogs. Betty heard the drawer to the desk slide open, and Finsch took something out. He once more crossed the floor, opened the door, departed.

On the other side of the door a key entered the lock, twisted. The lock snapped home.

Betty lay weakly back. Had he known she was there? Was he teasing her, tormenting her? She scrambled out from under the bed, went to the door and heard the heavy steps retreating down the corridor.

She tried the door. It was locked.

She turned away, heart in her mouth. She was caught. She looked at the porthole, wondering if she could wriggle out...Impossible.

She noted an object on the writing desk. Finsch's big black wallet. The reason he had locked the door.

Betty picked it up, opened it. The money compartment held a number of hundred-dollar bills. Tucked into a side pocket was a folded slip of paper, with a typewritten impression showing through. Betty opened it. It seemed to be a receipt, or a bill of sale, and was dated today. It read:

> Sold to Mik Finsch, for the sum of $3000, one slightly used wife, delivery at once, if not sooner.
>
> Alan J. Calder

Attached to the receipt was a check on the National Bank of El Salvador, for 7,500 *colones*, made out to Alan Calder and signed by Finsch. 7,500 *colones* was equivalent to three thousand dollars.

Betty could see the whole situation. Finsch had gone to dicker with Alan, intending to pacify him with a check. Then, after Isabelle's passage on the *Garda* had been secured, he would stop payment on the check. But Alan, not content with a symbolic payment, had refused to act until the check had cleared the bank. It was this particular snatch of conversation which Betty had heard at the window, immediately before the shot.

Why had Finsch kept the receipt and the check? Souvenirs? Dangerous souvenirs. Betty found a blank sheet of paper in the drawer, folded it to the size of the receipt, slipped it into Finsch's wallet, returned the wallet to its place on the desk. The receipt and the check she tucked into her own pocket. A reckless thing to do, thought Betty — reckless and very dangerous. No one knew her whereabouts. Finsch would be returning very soon. He was not a gentleman...Well, there was no help for it: back under the bed, and hope that she could avoid sneezing, as comedians in movies never seemed able to manage. Betty crouched down on her marrow-bones, slid back under the bed. What would Mother say if she could see her now?

Minutes passed; three, four, five. She heard the measured thud of Finsch's footsteps. The lock clicked, snapped back. The door opened, Finsch entered.

He hung up his towel, dropped the soap into its dish, returned his bathrobe to the closet. The odor of soapy flesh permeated the room. The thick hairy legs approached the bed, the feet flexed. A hand reached under the bed, slid out the suitcase. Both hands opened the lid; Betty stared in fascination at the big fingers. Finsch took a set of underwear from the suitcase. The jade ball stuck to the fabric, was lifted along with the underwear, and swung underneath as a pendulum. Finsch gave a grunt of surprise.

He stood up, and Betty could see only his feet, motionless. She heard him grunt again, softly, and mutter a word in a language unknown to her. He reached into his suitcase, came up with the packet of papers. Betty heard him leafing through them; then he tossed them back into the suitcase.

The big feet paced up and down the floor, once, twice — then stopped short in front of the bed. Betty's heart, already in her mouth, seemed to swell. Now he would find her...The right foot raised, the underwear flicked down, the left foot stepped through. Finsch went to the closet, and the process was repeated with his tan shorts.

A tap at the door. It opened without waiting for his summons. Slim sun-bronzed legs in white sandals entered.

Finsch asked casually, "Have you been in my room?"

Isabelle's voice was surprised and petulant. "In your room? Not since yesterday. Why?"

"Because someone has been here. My things have been disturbed."

Isabelle's legs moved two easy paces forward. "Are you sure?"

"Certainly. Look! My jade talisman. It is broken, and has been repaired...No, don't touch. See here? I will find out who is guilty. These are fingerprints, very clear in this place. Do you see?"

"Yes...I see. I wonder..."

"I wonder also. But I will find out. Notice," said Finsch in a slightly different voice, "notice that my pistol has been stolen."

"Mik!" exclaimed Isabelle in alarm. "What does that mean?"

"I do not know. It may be very good."

"Good?"

"Ha ha, aha!" exclaimed Finsch wisely, as if to imply that Isabelle not worry her head over such trifles.

"You're keeping something from me," said Isabelle in a nettled tone. "You're too pleased with yourself."

"I? Pleased with myself? My dear lady, not at all. I am only happy that affairs work out so smoothly."

"I still don't have my ticket."

"Ah, but there is no worry as to that. Alan will bring it this evening. If he does not, then we will wait until Panama."

"If you say so." Isabelle's feet moved slowly forward, stopped in front of Finsch's, then raised slightly up on the toes. Finsch's feet turned outwards. Betty squirmed, closed her eyes. It would be too much if they decided to become amorous!

They paid no heed to Betty's qualms. Isabelle's garments fell to the floor, her feet disappeared and the bed sagged under her weight. Finsch joined her and the bed sagged still further. Betty lay numb, paralyzed with embarrassment. It occurred to her that if she quietly crawled out from under the bed and left the room, Finsch would be too astonished to stop her, perhaps too engrossed even to notice. She choked back a titter.

There was nothing to do but wait. Time passed. Finsch and Isabelle lay quietly. Isabelle said, "Woof. I'm warm. All over sticky."

Finsch said nothing. Isabelle's feet appeared.

"I've got to rinse off. I can't live with myself."

"There is plenty time," said Finsch lazily.

"Not for me. You're cold-blooded, you can stand the heat." She dressed herself. "I'll meet you downstairs in ten minutes. It's the coolest place on the ship. You can buy me a drink, for a change."

"Very well. Today I will buy you a drink."

Isabelle slipped out of the room. Finsch lay on the bunk, hissing softly through his teeth. Presently he threw his legs over the side of the bed, stood up with the air of a man who has come to a decision. He dressed himself, went to the door. The door opened and closed. Betty waited. The lock clicked. Betty relaxed with a soft whimper of disappointment.

She crawled from under the bed, went to the door, looked at it. She tried the knob. The door was locked. She went to the porthole. Impossible.

There was a long wait ahead. Unless she pounded on the door, or yelled from the porthole. But she couldn't do it. There would be sniggers and whispers from the crew, elaborate understanding from the Catos, veiled mockery from Nello, jocularity from Harry. From Finsch and Isabelle…It was impossible. She must wait. Finsch might return before dinner, or he might not. In any case he would probably take care to lock the door after himself. Not until late in the evening, late at night, after Finsch had fallen asleep, could she hope to escape. A dismal prospect. On the verge of tears Betty sank upon the bed. What a day. What a terrible day.

She sighed mournfully, rose to her feet. Back under the bed. At any minute Finsch might return for something he had forgotten…Betty glanced at her hiding place with vast dislike. If only she could get out! She'd never snoop again! Never! If only she had a key — another key… There were two keys to Cabin #2. Perhaps there were two keys for Finsch's cabin. She opened the drawer to the desk. Far to the back she found a second key.

She seized it, ran to the door. If it failed to fit…She refused to think. She twisted, the lock turned over.

Betty opened the door a crack. The corridor was empty. She stepped out, closed and locked the door, walked away as fast as she could.

# 2

Betty climbed to the top deck, collapsed into a deck-chair. What a mess! And through no slightest fault of her own, she was in it up to her eyeballs! Well, she was going to get out from under, as soon as she could find the captain. Perhaps he was back on board now. She hauled herself to her feet, marched down to the captain's cabin.

She knocked. There was no answer. She knocked again, then opened the door, looked in. The office was empty. "Captain?" she called.

There was no answer.

Betty went to the wheel-house, which was vacant, then down the ladder to the boat deck, where she found the second mate, a middle-aged man with a long sad face and a limp ginger mustache, leaning on the rail.

"The captain — where is *il commandante*?"

The mate pointed toward the shore, explained in a mixture of Italian, Spanish and English.

"What time does he come back?"

The second mate held out his hands in a Latin gesture signifying ignorance and unconcern.

"Damn it to hell," said Betty under her breath. Wait. She had spent the entire day waiting. For the launch to shore, on the terrace of the hotel, in the warehouse, under Finsch's bed. Now here.

The pressure of so many irritations and frustrations demanded an outlet. Fury boiled inside of her. She was ripe for rebellion, ready to throw things. The second mate had turned away, and, wistfully sucking at his mustache, leaned on the rail. Betty's foot twitched, she ached to kick the plump bottom…Why not? He might be surprised and annoyed, but never again would he turn his back on anyone with such languid carelessness.

The mate slowly turned his head; he and Betty looked eye to eye for a moment, each reading something of the other's thoughts. The mate turned his melancholy gaze back toward the shore, and Betty walked away.

She wandered nervously around the ship — forward to the bow, aft to the fantail, then up to the top deck. She tried to settle in a deck-chair, but found it impossible to sit still. She jumped up, went out onto the wing of the flying bridge, watched anxiously for the launch. It might either bring the captain or the police — unless, of course, no one had thought to check into Alan's whereabouts. Betty stared up toward the hotel. She had only heard the shot — but really, there could be no doubt. When the police learned of Alan's death, they would want to know who had visited him. Enrique would describe Betty and her departure. The police could not fail to trace her to the *Garda*.

Still, Betty had nothing to fear but inconvenience. In her pocket she carried the bill of sale for 'one slightly-used wife, delivery at once, if not sooner' — bitter humor, that last! — and the check. She knew that the gun, rather than falling into the swirling sea, had lodged in a crevice. The police might be annoyed, but she would plead girlish nerves: no falsehood either! The girlish nerves were real! In any event, as soon as the captain appeared she would take him into his office. She would tell her story, give him the receipt and the check, describe where the gun lay. Captain Frascatore could take it from there. Of course, if the police arrived first she was sunk. They'd take her too. And the *Garda* sailed at midnight.

Here came the launch, now. Betty strained her eyes. Who was aboard?

The launch drew closer. Two men in uniform stood stern and rigid on the deck. Betty's heart took a queer hop. Beyond any question, the police.

The launch was alongside, the policemen came aboard, disappeared from sight. Betty stood indecisive, her knees shaking. What should she do? There was no one to turn to; the captain was ashore; she was alone… She took a deep breath. There was no cause for panic. If they took her ashore — they took her ashore.

She waited. Five minutes passed. She heard the launch roar away. She ran out on the wing of the flying bridge. The two police officers were departing — with Isabelle. She seemed frightened; she looked back toward the *Garda* with a white wild face.

Evidently, thought Betty, they had found Alan's body, and had come to notify Isabelle. But why would they take her ashore? To make funeral arrangements? Isabelle naturally would not wish to remain in La Libertad. They would think her very strange, very heartless.

Time passed. The sun slanted toward the sea, glittering on the water. Thick clouds gathered over the mountains, advanced over the town and began to unload tons of black rain. Betty sat in the deck-chair waiting and thinking.

At six o'clock Finsch appeared. He nodded politely, the humorous twist of his lips producing an effect of genial good-nature. Not to be outdone Betty nodded back. Finsch walked out on the flying bridge, lit a cigar and stood with feet spread apart, hands clasped behind his back, looking with benign approval over the sea. Presently he pulled a deck-chair around, settled himself.

After five minutes Betty began to feel fidgety. Finsch seemed to be watching her, speculating, calculating. She rose to her feet and went below.

With nothing better to do, she rinsed out a few underclothes, hung them up to dry. Then she went down to the mess-hall to wait for dinner or the captain, whichever came first.

# 3

The captain failed to return before dinner. Four new passengers appeared: a pair of middle-aged German engineers, a short pompous gray-haired Salvadorean and his plum-faced wife. The steward placed them at the table vacated by the four Salvadorean ladies. Betty occupied her usual place, Finsch ate in solitude at the table to the rear; the chief engineer sat at the center table, also alone. The meal was very quiet, except for a few mutters of conversation among the new passengers.

At nine o'clock Alec, Ora, Harry and Nello returned, tired, hot and hungry. They greeted Betty with surprise.

"I decided to stay aboard," said Betty. "You're stuck with me."

"Couldn't arrange a stop-over?" inquired Alec.

"It's a long story."

"Tell us later," said Ora. "We're starving. Alec, make them give us something to eat!"

The chief steward opened the refrigerator, brought out bread, butter, cheese, ham and salami, olives, pickles and tomatoes. Betty sat with them while they ate, and listened, rather wistfully, to their adventures.

Afterwards the five went up to the top deck, now cool and beautiful, to watch the stars and the lights of La Libertad.

At ten-thirty Captain Frascatore and Isabelle returned to the ship. Betty slipped away from the others and went below. She met Isabelle in the passage. Isabelle looked drawn and miserable; she walked past without a word, entered the cabin, shut the door.

Betty found the captain in his cabin, talking to the chief mate and chief engineer in Italian, with abrupt cuts of the hand and strokes of the fist. She tapped on the panel of the open door. "Captain, may I speak to you?"

Captain Frascatore looked tired and rumpled and out of sorts. He said, without friendliness, "Later, later."

"This is important, Captain."

"I am busy with my officers. We must get under way. There is ship's business to attend to."

"I've got to talk to you!" said Betty desperately.

Captain Frascatore became red in the face. He turned his head deliberately, uttered a vehement sentence or two to the mate and the chief engineer. They shrugged, nodded, took their leave. "Now — what is it?"

"May I ask, have you seen Alan Calder?"

"What about him?"

"Is he — dead?"

The captain pushed himself back in his chair. "Yes. He is dead." He looked away, out the porthole. "He killed himself. All day I have been working, doing Alan's work, so that tonight we may leave."

"Did you say, he killed himself?"

"I do not say. The police say. He is dead. A bullet in his head, a gun in his hand. They ask me why. I say, his wife runs off with Mik Finsch. They say, too bad."

"Captain," said Betty in a low hurried voice, "it wasn't that way at all. Alan didn't kill himself. Alan was killed!"

Captain Frascatore eyed her with dislike.

"I can prove it," said Betty. "Look here!" She took papers from her pocket. The captain suddenly threw up his hands.

"No no!"

Betty stared at him in astonishment.

"Do not show me. I want to know nothing. The ship must sail. If you want to talk, you talk to the police. You may go ashore. I do not want to hear."

"But Captain, Alan was murdered!"

"Do you know how much it costs to run this ship? No? Thirteen hundred dollars for one day. I do not want the *Garda* held in port. The police do not pay me to wait. The Mediterranean Line pays. They ask me, 'Captain Frascatore, why do you allow such trouble for the *Garda*?

You have cost us much money. I think we don't need you.' That is what they say to me. In three years I will retire. I will have a pension, unless they tell me I am no good."

"But — won't you look at these things?" Betty held out the papers, almost in tears. "It's not right that you shouldn't. Alan was murdered; I know where the gun is."

"Then why did you not tell the police?"

"I was afraid to."

Captain Frascatore slammed the table with his hand. "But you want me to tell them these things. They say, 'Captain Frascatore, what is this? You say that Alan Calder was murdered? How do you know?' I say, 'Miss Haverhill has told me.' 'Ah,' they say, 'she is a woman of sound judgment, eh?' I say, 'No, she is an excited young girl who already has made much trouble.' 'Ha hah!' they say, 'we are surprised, Captain Frascatore. We think you are a wise man, but you run to us like a chicken, very fast, because Miss Haverhill has an excitement.'" The captain threw out his hands, cocked his eyebrows, pursed his lips. "Then they say, 'If Miss Haverhill desires to speak to us, we must listen. That is our job. But we are satisfied with our investigation. We are good policemen.'"

Betty, almost beside herself with wrath, pushed the receipt and check across the table. "I'm *not* excited! These are facts! It proves what I say!"

The captain sat back. "Perhaps. But they are not my papers. It is no business of mine."

"But — Alan was killed, Captain!"

"Do not tell me things like this! Why did you not tell the police? You are afraid. You want *me* to tell. I am afraid too. You are afraid of the jail and the policemen. That is nothing. I am afraid of my pension. That is very much. I tell you what you must do. We must stay in Panama three days. You must go to the El Salvador Consul. You tell him. He will call the Italian Consul, who will call the police. Then there is time for an investigation."

Betty blinked back tears. "All you're telling me is that you don't care!"

"It is not whether I care — it is you who has the papers. You! Do you want to go ashore? I will call the launch. You can talk to the police."

"Yes," said Betty in a flash of anger. "I want to go ashore. I don't care what happens. I won't allow that man to get away with murder!"

"Good." The captain put his hands flat on the table, as if to jump to his feet. "I call the launch, you will go ashore. But I do not wait. When you are on the launch I raise the anchor. You tell the police what you wish. The *Garda* is gone."

"What good does it do me to go ashore?" cried Betty furiously. "You're deliberately —"

The captain spread out his hands. "These papers may say something. I do not believe, but maybe. The police say, 'This is very bad. We must investigate. Captain Frascatore, you must not sail until we find out everything. Tomorrow is the Lord's day, we may not investigate. Monday is fiesta. Tuesday is the saint's day of my nephew. Wednesday we will come aboard the *Garda* for the investigation.'" The captain slapped the table. "Each day is thirteen hundred dollars."

"But you're protecting a murderer!"

"No. It was not me who knew about these things. It was you. You do not take trouble, you want *me*, Captain Frascatore, to take trouble. But now you must wait."

Betty sank back in her chair. She looked numbly at the two bits of paper. "What about these? They are evidence."

The captain shrugged. "Perhaps. I do not know. If you like, you may put them in an envelope. I will keep them in a safe place."

Betty tried to think. It seemed as if every avenue was blocked. "I'll wait until we get to Panama. When will that be?"

"Three days from now. You do not wish to go ashore?"

"No. Give me the envelope."

The captain opened a drawer, withdrew an envelope.

Betty sealed the papers inside. The captain handed her a pen. "Write your name, please."

He watched her with cold curiosity. Face averted, she handed him the envelope. He snorted. "You are angry with me. But today I do you a favor."

"A favor? How?"

"There is a waiter at the hotel. He tells that a girl has come to see Alan, but she runs away very fast. The police they think it is the wife. So they make the waiter come to look at Mrs. Calder. He says, 'No, it is not the same girl!' I, Captain Frascatore, know that this girl is Miss Betty Haverhill. I say nothing. The police are tired. It is time for the siesta. This girl does not matter. Alan Calder is dead. He has a gun in his hand, he has a hole in his head. It is clear. The gun has made the hole. A man with a wife like this! 'Ay, caramba!' they say, 'when she leaves him, he is feeling bad. He shoots his head. It is an easy matter.' Now they drink beer. They wish Mrs. Calder were there to drink too. That is all they care. El Salvador, bah!"

The captain rose to his feet, took the envelope to a cabinet. "So, I lock this away."

A subdued clank sounded from the forward part of the ship. "That is the anchor," said the captain. "We are under way. I must go to the bridge."

# Chapter IX

## 1

THE GARDA MOVED OUT into the dark ocean and La Libertad fell astern, a few dozen lights shifting, dwindling, finally disappearing behind a projecting arm of land.

Betty went to the cabin, undressed and got into her pajamas. Isabelle and Mik Finsch still sat on the top deck. Betty hesitated a moment by the door, then shot the bolt. Feeling happier she brushed her teeth and lay down on the bed with a book. The print conveyed no meaning. Betty put the book aside and lay quietly, listening to the slide of the water along the hull.

Presently there was a step in the corridor; the door-knob turned. Betty went to the door. "Who is it?"

"It's me, naturally." Isabelle's voice was peevish.

Betty opened the door, peered out into the corridor. Isabelle was alone. She pushed in, looking suspiciously around the room. "What's the idea locking the door?"

"Call it a whim," said Betty, twisting the bolt.

"Again?" asked Isabelle sardonically.

"Yes."

"The same whim?"

Betty returned to bed. "If you want the truth — I'm scared."

"Scared?" Isabelle seemed surprised. "Scared of what?"

"Scared of committing suicide, as it's called on the *Garda*."

Isabelle sat on her bed, looked across at Betty. "What do you mean by that?"

"I'd rather not say."

Isabelle's beautiful gray eyes sparkled. "I'd rather you did say! I'm widow to a man who committed suicide, and I'm just a little sensitive."

Betty searched Isabelle's face. The indignation seemed real. "Do you really believe that your husband killed himself?"

"Why shouldn't I believe it? The police told me."

Betty took up her book. It was wiser to say nothing.

Isabelle sat motionless watching her. Betty pretended to read. The tension increased. Betty nervously turned a page.

"Just what are you hinting?" asked Isabelle gently.

"Isn't it clear that Alan didn't commit suicide?"

Isabelle stared at her with eyes bright as silver coins. "No," she said flatly. "It isn't clear. That's what the police told me. I believed them. I still do."

"Well, you're wrong," said Betty, in spite of her resolution to say no more. "Alan was shot and killed."

Isabelle's brows contracted slightly; otherwise her face did not change. After a moment she said flatly, "You seem pretty sure."

"I should think it's obvious."

"And who, then, did the shooting?"

Betty shrugged. "Draw your own conclusions."

Again the pause while Isabelle stared at her. "What you're telling me is that Mik shot Alan and made it look like suicide."

"I'm not telling you a thing."

Isabelle's response was swift and definite. "Yes, you are. And you're crazy."

"Just as you say."

Isabelle took a quick step across the room. Betty drew up her knees, ducked away. But Isabelle merely stood looking down with a faint smile on her face. "I know why you're telling me this."

"I'm not telling you anything."

"Because you're jealous."

"Jealous?" asked Betty wonderingly. "Of what?"

"When I came aboard at Los Angeles, Mik dropped you like a hot potato." Betty spluttered an indignant denial. Isabelle laughed. "I know all about it. Mik told me."

"Did he tell you that I was trying to get away from him, that he was sitting on me, tearing my clothes off?"

Isabelle laughed again, scornfully.

"Did he tell you that Ted Bunpole came in and gave him a good beating? No. He wouldn't tell you that. Ted Bunpole also committed suicide."

"Ha ha." The laugh was a trifle less assured. "Isn't all this rather melodramatic?"

"It certainly is! I wish it weren't! I'd rather be bored stiff."

Isabelle went back to the bed. "I'd like to ask you a question."

"Go ahead."

"Do you have anything definite to go on — about Alan — or are you just talking?"

Betty considered. "I didn't actually see the shot fired, if that's what you mean."

Isabelle leaned forward suddenly. "I know now! It must have been you! *You* were the girl who came to see Alan!"

"What of it?"

"What of it! The police thought it was me!"

Betty shrugged. "I told the captain I was there."

Isabelle eyed her with aversion, wonder and a tinge of respect. "You're a cool one, aren't you? No wonder you know all about everything."

"I don't know all about everything," said Betty sulkily.

"But you heard the shot."

"Yes."

"How do you know that Alan didn't shoot himself?"

"I'd rather not say. I told everything I know to the captain."

"And he didn't believe you?"

"He thinks I'm a hysterical young girl."

Isabelle nodded with a slight smile, as if she found the captain's opinion quite understandable. "What it amounts to is you heard Alan shooting himself."

"No," said Betty positively.

"My dear girl," said Isabelle in a tired voice, "Alan had a gun in his hand. There was a bullet fired. And he left a note."

"On the typewriter?"

"So what?"

Now Betty laughed. "You're not that dumb, Isabelle. If you don't believe me, it's because you don't want to believe."

"Or maybe," said Isabelle softly, "because I just don't care."

"I've told you," said Betty. "I didn't intend to, but I did." She picked up her book, tried to read.

After a moment Isabelle said, "I just can't figure you out. Did you see Mik up there?"

"No."

"Did you hear his voice?"

"No."

"Then how do you know he was there?"

"Something Alan said."

"May I ask what?"

"Really, Isabelle, I'd rather not talk about it!"

"Why not? After all, Alan was my husband. I won't pretend I'm all broken up — but still I've got a right to know."

"Because everything I tell you you'll run and tell Finsch."

Isabelle laughed in brittle fashion. "What you say is ridiculous in the first place. Look, if Mik shot Alan with Alan's gun —"

"He used his own gun."

"Well then — if he used his own gun, how is it there's a shot fired from Alan's gun? You only heard one shot."

"Maybe there was an empty cartridge already in Alan's gun. Maybe Finsch wrapped the gun in a blanket and fired it, so it made no noise. There must be a dozen ways. Finsch was in the secret police, he must know them all." She picked up her book and tried to read once more. She had already told Isabelle far more than she had intended; far more than might be — safe.

The words ran together; presently she put down her book, pulled the cord on her bed lamp. Isabelle already had turned out her own light, but Betty knew that she was not asleep. Betty asked presently, "Aren't you at all concerned?"

Isabelle's voice came sweet and calm through the dark. "No. Because I don't believe you."

"You don't *want* to believe me."

There was a silence. Both girls lay staring into the dark. The engines throbbed dully, far away. The ship rose slowly to the swells, nosed down, slid forward. Through the porthole came the hiss of the passage, the great hull sliding through the water.

# 2

Next morning found the *Garda* out of sight of land, pitching in a choppy sea. A strong wind blew freakishly from the east, out of Nicaragua, bringing ragged gray clouds and spatters of warm rain. Breakfast was a dour affair. Ora had become sea-sick, or perhaps something she had eaten in San Salvador had disagreed with her; at any rate she made no appearance. Harry Mayberry had risen from the wrong side of the bed; he and Nello already had quarreled over some triviality. Now both sat sulking over their coffee: Harry pink and pouting, a kewpie doll in an outrageous pet, his white hair fluffy and disarranged; Nello savagely tearing a slice of toast to pieces. The German engineers muttered in monosyllables, the Salvadorean couple covertly watched Finsch and Isabelle, who finished quickly and left the mess-hall. Alec likewise excused himself in order to see to Ora, Nello came to sit beside Betty. Harry Mayberry rose to his feet, stalked from the room.

Nello explained the background of the dispute. "He is old, that Harry, but he knows nothing. I speak of d'Annunzio; he knows nothing. I say Garibaldi; he knows nothing. Cavour? Ignorance. Then I say, 'Harry, my friend, it is unbelievable! At least you have heard of Joe DiMaggio.' He becomes angry. It is strange, the Americans are a strange people."

"All people are strange," said Betty.

Nello reached out his hand, stroked Betty's wrist. "You are pale. Are you feeling well?"

"I'm feeling very well."

"When we get to Panama, you and I, we go out together. What do you say?"

Betty laughed sharply. "I might not even reach Panama."

"I think you must rest today," said Nello. "You did not sleep well last night, no?"

"I slept very well. Really, Nello! You'll give me an inferiority complex if you keep on worrying."

"But I must worry. I am in love with you. You look so pretty and so innocent, like a box of lovely bon-bons wrapped in the nicest paper."

"Thank you, Nello. I'm sure you mean well."

"I have said something wrong?"

"Nothing serious. Girls don't want to be told they look innocent."

"Ah, I understand. Better if I say that you do not look innocent."

"That's wrong too."

Nello clutched his head, raised his hands in fine Italian frenzy. "Never will I understand!"

Betty stood up, went to the porthole. "What a dismal day! Nello, think of something amusing."

"Let us plan what we will do in Panama."

"Come along, we'll visit Ora. Maybe she's feeling better."

Nello made a sour face. "I am not interested. Mrs. Ora Cato has a sharp tongue. Why do you not go yourself?"

"I'm afraid of the dark."

"Dark?" Nello looked at Betty curiously. "It's not dark."

"You have a literal mind, Nello. I'm speaking in poetic images."

"I cannot understand."

"It doesn't matter. Are you coming?"

"Oh, if you wish." He followed Betty along the corridor, up the stairs. Sharp steel stairs, thought Betty — terrible things to fall down.

The Catos' cabin was empty. "They're up on top," said Betty. "First I'll get my sweater."

They went to Cabin #2. Betty opened the door. Isabelle, standing in the middle of the cabin, hastily closed Betty's purse. Betty stopped short, nonplussed. "What goes on?"

"Don't jump to conclusions," said Isabelle in a throaty voice. "Your money's safe. I thought I'd try your lipstick."

Stranger and stranger! thought Betty. Towels, soap, talcum, toothpaste, shower-cap, all these articles and commodities Isabelle had at one time or another appropriated for her own use. Now lipstick. What next?

Betty threw her hands up fatalistically, took her sweater and left the cabin. She joined Nello, they went up to the top deck.

Ora sat huddled like a wet chicken. Alec slouched morosely beside her. Betty pulled up a chair beside Ora. "It's not very cheerful today, is it?"

"No," said Ora peevishly. "It's windy and damp and I'm miserable. Those damn taco things Alec insisted on buying — they did it. I've caught amoebic dysentery, and I'll be sick the rest of my life."

Alec glared indignantly. "Come now, let's be reasonable. The beer upset you. Green beer can be dynamite."

"I don't care what it was. Let's talk of something more cheerful."

Alec heaved himself forward, peered curiously at Betty. "We've been meaning to ask, did you see Alan Calder yesterday?"

"No; as a matter of fact —" The room steward leaned over her shoulder. "Please, the captain, he wants to see you."

Betty excused herself, went down to the captain's cabin.

The door was open. She saw Captain Frascatore sitting behind his table, grim and haggard. Isabelle and Mik Finsch sat to the right of the door. Finsch rose politely as Betty entered. The captain waved his hand to a chair, holding his eyes away from Betty.

Betty sat down; Finsch resumed his seat.

There was a moment's silence. The captain fidgeted with some loose sheets of paper. Isabelle stared stonily at the porthole. Finsch's half-smile was quizzical, almost impish. Something was in the wind, thought Betty. "Well, I'm here," she said, her voice shaking slightly. "What's up?"

The captain put his palms down flat on his table. "This is not a nice business. I do not like it on the *Garda*. Mr. Finsch has made a complaint to me. It is very unpleasant."

Mik Finsch spoke in the most reasonable of voices. "I regret this matter very much, Miss Haverhill. It is unpleasant for me. But I cannot allow property to be taken from my cabin. Surely you can understand that. But let us choose the easy way. I want no trouble for anyone. If you will give my automatic pistol to me, I will say no more."

Betty looked in astonishment from Finsch to the captain, back to Finsch. "I don't have your automatic pistol."

"Ah, Miss Haverhill!"

"And you know very well I don't have it."

"As I say, I wish no trouble. We are talking now between friends. If you give me my gun, then we will forget all about it."

"I don't have your gun — for a very good reason!"

"But you must have," protested Finsch, his half-smile trembling with charm and persuasiveness. "You came into my cabin, you opened my suitcase, you took my gun. All this I know."

Betty leaned back in her chair, looking from Finsch to Isabelle. Finsch waited patiently. Isabelle would not meet her gaze. Betty smiled bitterly. Isabelle naturally had repeated everything. The chips were down now. But Betty had nothing to worry about. Her position was unassailable. "Out of curiosity," said Betty, "why should I steal your gun?"

It was the wrong question to ask, for it gave Finsch his opening. "I do not know why you took my gun, but you did. That is the fact. I saw it Friday night. That is the night before last. Mrs. Calder had come to my cabin for a drink. She will verify it was there then."

"Yes," said Isabelle in a strained quick voice. "The gun was there Friday night. I saw it."

"This morning I notice it is gone. You took it yesterday morning, after I had gone ashore for my luggage."

Betty laughed huskily. "The gun is gone, Mik Finsch — but I didn't take it. You took it yourself."

"I am sorry, Miss Haverhill. The gun is missing and I can prove that you were in my suitcase between these times I have mentioned. You broke a very valuable antique, and you tried to conceal this fact. One can be too clever. You have revealed yourself." He pointed to an object folded into a clean white handkerchief. "There is my jade, a talisman, very valuable. It has been broken and clumsily cemented together. Mrs. Calder tells me you carry this kind of cement. Is that correct?"

Betty bit her lip. The captain was watching her carefully. It was awkward. Finsch was making her out a sneak-thief and a liar. In contrast to his untroubled good-nature, she must seem furtive and scheming. She must recover her poise, make her denial sound as convincing as Finsch's courteous accusations. She attempted a tone of contemptuous disdain. "Certainly I carry cement with me. That proves nothing whatever."

"True," admitted Finsch readily. "Anyone may carry cement. But only you can leave your fingerprints. That is proof! Look!" He unfolded the handkerchief. "Look! There is the ball. It is broken. This is the crack. This spot is cement which was not wiped off. The white is talcum powder. Do you see this excellent fingerprint? It is preserved in the cement."

Betty stared wordlessly. Her face was pale, her eyes big with consternation. She looked at the fingerprint, started to speak, but Finsch judiciously held up his big white hand. "Perhaps I am wrong. I do not think so, but it is possible. You may disprove me. I hope you will. I do not like to embarrass pretty girls. You need only show us your fingerprints. Here is paper, here is a stamp pad. You can make good fingerprints, and show me that I am wrong. If you will, please."

Betty drew back. "I'll do nothing of the sort."

Finsch shrugged, looked at the captain.

The captain leaned forward, fixed Betty with an unfriendly gaze. "This is a very bad position. I am obliged to believe that —"

"For heaven's sake!" Betty burst out. "Can't you see what he's doing? He's pulling a red herring in front of your nose!"

The captain became a trifle flushed. "I do not know. Let us look at the facts. This gun, it is an important matter. Alan Calder is shot. The police say it is suicide, but I do not think so. You are at the hotel. I know it is you, but I do not tell the police. Maybe I am wrong. I do not want the *Garda* held in port. I think that you have nothing to do with Alan Calder. Why should you shoot Alan? But now Mr. Finsch says you steal his gun. He has your fingerprints. I think, maybe there are more things here than I know about. I think, this little Miss Haverhill, she takes old Captain Frascatore as a fool."

"Can't you see the truth? It's as plain as the nose on your face! Finsch shot Alan Calder, and we all know he did! Why pretend anything different?"

Finsch shook his head gravely, brought a cigar from his pocket. "That is a serious thing to say, Miss Haverhill. Of course I did not shoot Alan Calder, and it cannot be proved that I did." He put the cigar in his mouth, lit it.

"We'll see about that. I know where you threw the gun. I saw it come out of the window. I know where it is now."

Finsch spoke sharply. "So. You know where someone threw a gun. Could it be that you threw it yourself?"

Betty laughed. "This is absolutely insane. Why should I shoot Alan? I went to see him because life with Isabelle is intolerable. She's selfish and immoral, doesn't wash her underwear, and half a dozen other things. I wanted to take passage on another ship. Why should I shoot Alan? He's the man who could help me!"

"But this is not reasonable," argued Finsch. "Because here you still are on the ship."

Betty smiled bitterly. "You got to Alan before I did. If I hadn't been such a coward, I would have told the police."

Finsch shook his head reproachfully. "That is the second time you have accused me. It is a serious thing to say to a man. Of course, it is so ridiculous. Why should I shoot poor Alan?"

"Because of her."

"That is where you are the most unreasonable. We are men and women of the world. Let us admit that Alan might want to shoot me. That is understandable. But I shoot him? No. It is not true to life."

Betty began to feel panicky. Would anyone believe her? If Finsch could convince the authorities that Betty took his gun... She thought of the receipt and the check. "You did not see Alan at all, then?"

"Of course not."

"You heard that?" Betty asked the captain, who grunted uncomfortably. "I can prove you saw Alan Calder! In his own handwriting. And in your handwriting too."

Finsch's eyes glittered; the corners of his mouth drew back to show the shine of his teeth. "I would like to see this proof."

"You will — don't worry about that!"

"May I ask what sort of proof you refer to? I will show you how it is wrong."

The captain's attention had shifted from Betty, he was now looking dubiously toward Finsch. He slapped his hands on the table. "We will settle this in Panama. There will be an inquiry, and we will find out the truth. It is a very bad trip for me. I do not like quarrels and troubles."

"It is difficult for all of us," said Finsch. "I will be glad to see things in order. I think Miss Haverhill is very young and perhaps a little hys-

terical. I would like my gun back. It is like an old companion. But —"
he shrugged, somberly puffed his cigar.

Betty rose to her feet. "Is that all you wanted, Captain?"

"That is all."

Betty marched back up to the top deck. To her annoyance her hands
were shaking and she felt sick to her stomach. Alec and Nello sat reading; Ora had gone below.

Betty went to the other side of the deck, sank into a chair, sat looking across the wind-whipped sea. Everything was gray: the sky, the sea,
the ship. She thought of home, the cheerful green and white house
under the oak trees; the familiar living room, the comfortable chairs,
the book shelves, the fireplace. Fervently she wished she were there.
Impossible. The *Garda* was a floating jail, moving with snail-like slow-
ness through the dreariest of oceans. This was the absolute low point of
her life. If only she could go to sleep, or get drunk... Isabelle came up
the stairs. She went to the rail, gripped it with her two hands, stared out
over the sea. She turned, looked toward Betty. Her face was white, her
eyes narrow, her mouth a pale tight line.

She came across the deck, four long steps, knees bent, unpleasantly
like a running insect. She stopped; Betty looked up in time to catch
a blur of motion. A shock, a dazed unreality, a stinging smart on the
cheek. Betty put her hand slowly to her cheek. Isabelle's face, fleshless
as a skull, blazed with white wrath.

"So I'm dirty and immoral; I'll tell you what you are." She told Betty
and Betty cringed. She had heard the words before, she knew what
they meant, but Isabelle used them with a spiteful nastiness that was
vastly shocking. Betty stared in appalled wonder. She put her legs to
the deck, started to rise; Isabelle pushed her back down into the seat,
and Betty no longer cared about anything. She punched Isabelle in the
stomach, kicked at her legs, rolled off the chair to the deck. Isabelle
ran over, kicked Betty's ribs, back, head. Betty caught Isabelle's ankle,
pulled. Isabelle hopped frantically backward into the rail. Betty staggered erect; Isabelle sprang at her, spitting like a cat, hands like talons.
Betty ran behind the chair, and Isabelle stumbled into it. Betty grabbed
her hair, pulled her forward; Isabelle fell face down across the chair.
Betty spanked the upturned rump, so hard her hand stung, twice, three

times. Isabelle, screaming, flung her arms around Betty's legs, bit her thigh. The feel of the teeth drove Betty frantic. She jerked up her knee, felt the hardness of Isabelle's head, lost her balance and fell beside the chair with Isabelle struggling down on top of her, biting, clawing, wailing curses. Confusion: glimpses of blonde hair, glaring gray eyes, open yelling mouth. Movement: up, down, strike, kick, pull, scratch. Sensation and shock, but no pain; urgency but no fear; an unfamiliar state of being beyond emotion.

Something tugged back at Betty. Isabelle was pulled away. Betty's eyes focused: Alec had seized Isabelle, Nello had wrapped his arms around her own waist. "Stop it, stop it!" Alec shouted. "For God's sake calm down! Relax! What are you trying to do, murder each other?"

The two girls stood panting and limp. The captain came running up from the bridge, red-faced with despairing anger. "What is this? What happens? What do you do?"

"She came up here and hit me!" cried Betty, tears of passion streaming down her cheeks. "I want a different cabin! I won't sleep in the same room with her!"

"There are no other cabins; I have enough of this foolishness! I care nothing for you! You can sleep where you are or on the deck."

"But —"

"No matter!" roared the captain. "There is no reason for this thing! Why do you not get along together? If there is anything more like this I lock you up for three days!"

"I'd just as soon," muttered Isabelle, her face white beneath its tan and dry as sun-bleached bone.

"No! It is impossible. You are ladies and gentlemen. You do not fight aboard the *Garda*! You have your cabin, you must sleep there. You need not speak, you need not look. But you must sleep. Mother of God, Santa Maria! What a trip!"

"What a trip is right!" Betty angrily thrust her elbows back. "Nello, will you stop breathing down my neck!"

"How can you feel me breathe in this wind?"

"Never mind how I feel you." Betty looked down at herself. She was bruised and dirty, her blouse was torn and her hair was tangled. She looked at Isabelle, who was in like case. "I'm going below and clean up."

"First," said the captain, "you must agree: no more fighting."

"Certainly I agree!" exclaimed Betty. "I never started this one!"

Isabelle nodded distantly. "I gave her what she deserved, that's all I care about."

"I went a lot easier on you," Betty retorted.

Alec laughed, even the captain grinned. Betty said shortly, "I'm going to clean up."

# 3

Betty took a shower, examined her bruises, dressed in fresh clothes. Isabelle came into the cabin; the air was stiff with hostility. Neither spoke, neither looked at the other.

Lunch was even more strained than breakfast. Nello had nothing to say, Ora kept to her cabin. Harry Mayberry still sulked, feeling further abused because he had missed the fight. The captain, stony and hostile, refused to lift his eyes from his plate, the chief engineer was no more sociable than ever. The new passengers darted curious glances around the room, muttering dubiously to each other. Betty and Alec exchanged brittle badinage, then abruptly became silent. Isabelle and Finsch spoke in undertones which seemed to Betty laden with dire malice. A murderer is sitting behind me, she told herself, with sudden surprise. A murderer! I take it for granted, that's the marvel! I sit here eating my lunch, he sits there eating his lunch! A murderer who hates me and fears me — otherwise he wouldn't have gone to the captain this morning. Isabelle of course spilt the beans; I talked too much, and now he's scheming.

Betty stirred the bitter Italian coffee, with a crawling at the back of her neck. The chair creaked as Finsch rose to his feet. "Now, a little siesta — the real dessert to lunch. Today is cooler."

Betty watched him leave the room. He almost filled the doorway. Heavy shoulders and hips, big muscular arms and hands. She turned soberly back to her coffee.

After lunch Betty and Alec went to look in at Ora. Outside the cabin, Alec signalled for silence, opened the door with the utmost caution.

"I'm not asleep and I'm not at death's door," came Ora's voice. "No need for all that elaborate pussy-footing."

"You have company," Alec told her. "Betty is here to visit you."

"Oh good. Come in."

Betty seated herself on Alec's bed, while Alec leaned against the wash-basin. Ora examined Betty carefully. "Alec tells me you had something of a tiff this morning."

Betty laughed self-consciously. "Just a little hair-pulling. Nothing serious." In retrospect the fight seemed almost fun. There had been a wide-open sensation, a wildness and abandon, that she had never known before.

Ora watched her with bird-like intentness. "How did it start?"

Betty described the events which led to the fight. To explain these, she reverted to the scene in the captain's cabin, which necessitated going into the matter of Alan Calder's death, and presently Betty found herself telling the entire story.

Ora was vastly impressed, and looked at Betty with new respect. "To think you've been keeping all this to yourself!"

Betty moved uneasily. "I feel rather foolish, running back here in a panic. I know I should have gone to the police."

"It's a harrowing position to find yourself in," said Ora sympathetically. "I don't know what I would have done."

"If it was harrowing then, it's worse now. I get simply stifled thinking about it!" She blew out her breath. "And this heat to boot!"

"It's especially hot in here," said Ora. "With typical Italian efficiency, our fan refuses to work."

There was a short silence. Betty heaved another melancholy sigh. "The worst of it is," she said, "I'm scared."

Alec raised his eyebrows. "Oh I hardly think it's come to that. If Finsch planned violence, he wouldn't have taken you before the captain. He realizes your testimony is damaging and he's trying to discredit you in advance."

"Yes, but then he didn't know I had the receipt and the check."

"Does he know it now?"

"I imagine he must. I had to shoot my mouth off."

Ora chuckled. "And he's wondering how in the world you got them."

Alec shook his head. "I don't see how the receipt and the check make too much difference. Finsch can make a fairly convincing case that you took his gun. Isabelle corroborates that the gun was in the suitcase and the jade ball in one piece before La Libertad, that the gun was gone and the jade ball broken after La Libertad. And the jade ball has your fingerprints on it."

"How could he be sure they were Betty's fingerprints?" Ora objected.

"A simple enough deduction."

"It doesn't sound simple to me," snapped Ora. "Why couldn't it have been someone else?"

"He knew approximately when the ball was broken. During this time all the rest of us were in San Salvador. Of course it's possible he only suspected, and found some means to verify his suspicion —"

Betty sat up straight on the bed. "I've been wondering about that too. Now I know. It's my right thumb-print on the jade, where I pressed the two halves together. Isabelle could easily have taken my driver's license from my purse. In fact, now that I think of it, I almost caught her in the act. She said she was borrowing my lipstick! She must have been putting it back! Anyway, it shows my right thumb-print, perfectly convenient for Mr. Mik Finsch. He *knew* I'd been in his suitcase."

Alec held up his hand. "Let me go on. My point is that the receipt and the check, in your possession, carry no great weight."

"I don't see why," said Betty. "They prove that —"

"Because there's only your word to connect them to Finsch. He can say, 'Certainly I went to see Alan. He demanded money, I gave it to him. We parted on good terms. Someone came in afterwards, shot Alan with my gun and took these papers. Betty Haverhill took my gun. Perhaps she shot Alan. I do not know.'"

Betty gave a bark of nervous laughter. "But why should I shoot poor Alan?"

"Silly, of course. Still — the physical evidence points to you as strongly as to Finsch. Even more strongly — because you were seen at the hotel and Finsch was not. By one interpretation of the evidence — yours — parsimony and resentment drove Finsch to kill. Finsch, of course, laughs this off. What are a few thousand *colones* to him? By his interpretation of the same evidence, you stole his gun and shot Alan. He does not know why. The girl is hysterical in the heat."

"Oh Alec, stop being so glib," exclaimed Ora. "It's irritating!"

"Excuse me, my dear. I find myself using my brain again."

Ora sighed, turned to Betty. "Never marry a man who fancies himself a wit. He'll crucify you."

Alec lit his pipe without comment. Ora sat up in bed. "We're all smothering in here. I've got to get out on deck, sick or not. That damn electric fan. I've complained to the captain, he says the electrician will fix it. The door sticks, the faucet drips —"

"In short, a hell-ship," said Alec. He opened the door. "We'll go on up."

# 4

"Ora is unusually truculent this morning," Alec remarked. "She's hungry, she's hot, she's sick to her stomach."

"That seems reason enough," said Betty.

"She also believes that she could design, construct, launch and operate a ship better than the *Garda* with her own hands."

Betty sighed mournfully. "I wish I were home."

Ora appeared and threw herself into a deck-chair. "Confounded ship. The latch on the bathroom is loose. Now we can't lock the door. I hope the propeller doesn't drop off."

Alec puffed his pipe. "There's material here for wonderful reminiscences."

Ora laughed grimly. "We won't forget this trip, no fear of that!"

"Those of us who survive," said Betty.

Alec smilingly shook his head. "So far as Finsch is concerned, it's your word against his. He only needs to sit tight and deny everything."

"Not necessarily," said Ora. "Suppose there's other evidence, which Finsch knows of, but which we've overlooked?"

"In that case, Finsch becomes a very dangerous man, of course."

"Exactly," said Ora.

Betty hugged herself as if she were cold. "I'm going to lock myself in the cabin and not come out till the ship docks."

Alec made an easy gesture with his pipe. "He can't shoot you without his gun; he can't poison you without conniving with the steward; he can't strangle you unless —"

"You're scaring the poor girl out of her wits!" snapped Ora.

"Yes, Alec." Betty was annoyed to hear the tremble in her voice. "You really are. I'm not brave."

Ora glared at Alec. "Of course you'll be safe. Just be careful. Fore-warned is fore-armed. And naturally we'll always be at hand."

"If there's any trouble, Ora will give Finsch a piece of her mind," said Alec.

"Quiet," said Ora. "Here he comes."

Finsch mounted the stairs, wearing tan shorts, a blue short-sleeved shirt, his broad-brimmed hat. He paused, looked back along the way the ship had come, then shaking his head critically, sauntered over to stand behind Ora. "Notice the wake of the ship. See how it is crooked? The man at the wheel does not know his work."

Ora twisted around in her chair. "Yes. We do seem to be wandering."

Finsch went to the rail, examined the sky. "Tonight there will be a very hard rain. That is how it comes this time of year. Tomorrow there will be sun and heat — the real heat of the tropics! Tomorrow you must eat salt, because tomorrow you will sweat!" He took off his hat, fanned himself. "Excuse me. I see the German engineers. It is many years since I spoke German; I am anxious to learn again."

He ambled across the deck, drew a chair up beside the two Germans. Betty saw him point aft to the wake, saw the Germans look back as Finsch explained the ineptitude of the quartermaster.

"Two days to Panama," said Betty. "Less than two days. Thirty-six hours."

"Don't worry," said Ora. "Just don't go anywhere alone. Lock the door to your cabin, and scream like blazes if he comes near you."

"What a trip," muttered Betty. "What a trip."

"Where's Isabelle?" asked Ora.

"I haven't seen her since lunch. She's usually with Finsch when she isn't taking a shower."

Ora sniffed. "I wouldn't dare, with the bolt the way it is. Anyone could walk right in on you. Alec, will you kindly report it to the captain? I'm not overly modest, but there are limits."

"Yes, dear. I'll make your complaints heard."

# 5

The day passed. The *Garda* heaved and plunged through the gray sea, leaving a confused white wake. Black frigate-birds soared astern, slid down to within inches of the water and away on a gust of wind. Under the heavy clouds, twilight came early. The wind dwindled to soft cool gusts, then died, and the ocean took on the look of varnished slate. With night came the rain, soft big drops at first, then a torrent dashing on the decks and into the ocean with an enormous hissing roar.

Dinner, like breakfast and lunch, was quiet. Ora put in a wan appearance, to pick at a piece of boiled chicken. Harry Mayberry, however, had succumbed to a similar malady and kept to his cabin. Betty ate scarcely more than Ora, conscious at all times of the man sitting eight feet behind her back.

After dinner, Alec, Ora, Nello and Betty played bridge, while the ship lifted over the low swells and the rain drove against the portholes. Finsch and Isabelle played a few hands of solitaire, each on his own side of the table. Finsch's half-grin was fixed; Isabelle seemed sullen and bored. Presently Finsch slapped the cards to the table in dissatisfaction, turned to the German engineers. They offered brandy, which Finsch accepted and Isabelle declined.

For half an hour Finsch and the engineers talked in German while Isabelle fretfully continued her solitaire.

The bridge game broke up after a single rubber, with no one sufficiently keen to urge another. There was nothing to do now but go to bed. Betty surreptitiously eyed Finsch where he sat drinking the brandy poured generously by the Germans. They seemed to find him a congenial companion, and leaned attentively forward to hear his stories.

Betty winced and shivered. I should ask the captain for protection. I should demand that a watch be kept on Finsch... She smiled bitterly, envisioning the captain's response to her request.

Ora swiveled around in her chair, stood up. "Bed-time. It's cool in the cabin and I shall read."

"I think I'll be off too," said Betty. Now was the time to go. Finsch, still drinking, could not possibly waylay her in the corridors. There was still her shower, but tonight, sticky or not, she would have to forego it.

Betty and Ora set off down the corridor, longer and dimmer tonight than ever. They climbed the steel stairs, and Ora stopped, for here their ways diverged. "You'll be all right now," said Ora, patting Betty's arm. "Lock your door and you'll be perfectly safe."

"I wish I had your confidence," said Betty. "For two cents I'd throw a good fit of hysterics."

"Oh ftt, ftt." This was a noise of deprecation and admonishment Ora made between her teeth. "Now you mustn't be silly."

Betty looked dubiously along the corridor. "I've half a mind to ask the captain to set a guard, or something of the sort."

Ora snorted. "He'd laugh at you."

"Yes. I suppose he would."

From below came the sound of hearty German voices. "Here he comes," said Ora. "You run along now."

"Goodnight."

"Goodnight and don't worry!"

Betty ran to Cabin #2, entered, flicked on the light, closed and locked the door. Standing in the center of the room she looked around her, in her mind some vague concern for booby-traps.

The cabin appeared normal. She peered under the bed, examined the closets, finding nothing to alarm her. So far, so good. With slightly more assurance she changed into pajamas, sat cross-legged on her bed, reading and listening. Fifteen minutes passed. Brisk footsteps sounded in the corridor. The door-knob twisted.

Betty went to the door. "Who is it?"

"It's me!" — Isabelle's voice, peevish and irritated.

Betty turned the bolt, eased the door open a crack. Isabelle impatiently pushed forward. Betty closed the door, turned the bolt.

Isabelle watched in amused contempt. "Still scared?"

"I don't trust your boyfriend," said Betty. "In fact, he's a murderer."

Isabelle shrugged. "You keep saying that; pretty soon you'll believe it." She sat on her bed, kicked off her sandals. "I'm sorry I started that fight, if it's any consolation to you."

"Oh well," said Betty, "it was partly my fault. I shouldn't have called you names. Not to your face anyway."

Isabelle paused in her undressing. "I don't know what got into me. It's the last thing I intended to do. I've nothing in the world to fight about, no troubles, no worries. For the first time in my life."

"That's nice."

Isabelle looked at Betty with a cool grin. "You've got yourself in a mix-up. Why did you break his ball? He's disturbed about that, more than anything else."

"Why did you take my driver's license, since we're asking questions?"

Isabelle shrugged. "He wanted to see it. It did no harm. If you're guilty, you're guilty; if you're not, you're not."

"I'm not guilty."

"You took Mik's gun. You can't deny that."

"Of course I deny it! I went into that suitcase after I got back aboard the ship. After I heard the shot, after I saw the gun go over the cliff. I wanted to make sure it was Finsch's gun. It was his, all right."

Isabelle took a deep breath. "I can't worry about it. I don't want to know."

"But suppose you knew for sure, for absolutely certain sure, that Finsch killed Alan —"

"Maybe Alan pulled a gun first."

"He wouldn't have done that. I heard them talking. Alan said something like, 'We'll take this check to the bank right now, we'll put it through right now!' And then came the shot. Finsch just didn't want to lose the money."

Isabelle made an annoyed noise in her throat. "I don't want to know these things. I want to forget the whole damn mess."

"Afraid to learn the truth?"

"I'm just not interested."

"Suppose you did know?"

"But I don't know."

"Just suppose."

Isabelle took a deep irritated breath. "I don't know what I'd do. What difference does it make? I don't approve of killing, if that's what you're getting at. If I knew for sure, for absolute sure, I'd quit him. But I don't know and I don't want anyone trying to convince me. I have faith in Mik. I won't listen to anything against him."

Betty heaved a deep sigh of relief. At the back of her mind had lurked the fear that Isabelle might assist Finsch, become his accomplice. Then Betty would have had no chance whatever.

"I'm afraid of him," said Betty with simple honesty. "Will you promise me you won't open the door or unlock it during the night?"

Isabelle burst into uneasy laughter. "You've really got the wind up."

Betty nodded. "Will you promise me?"

"If it'll make you feel any better." She noticed Betty's pajamas. "Aren't you taking a shower tonight?"

"No."

"Now I know you're scared. You're a pretty regular kid. Like clockwork. Up at seven, brush teeth. After dinner, take shower, brush teeth, go to bed."

"Tonight it's just brush teeth. I'm not stirring out of this room."

"Well, I'm going to take a shower. I'm all sticky. I can't stand it. I don't know how you can."

Betty shrugged. "Ten minutes after a shower I'm sticky again. I just don't bother. Not tonight anyway."

"It's hot and wet tonight, and that's when I really sweat." Isabelle stepped out of her clothes, wrapped herself in her white bathrobe. "If I can't unlock the door, how am I going to take my shower?"

"I'll let you out. When you want to come back in, knock twice."

"You're not taking any chances, are you?"

"I hope not. I think your boyfriend wants to kill me."

Isabelle took the red shower-cap hanging on the towel-rack. "Mik is harmless as a teddy bear. I twist him around my finger." She pulled the shower-cap down over her blonde hair. My shower-cap, thought Betty, too weary to protest.

She went to the door, put her hand on the bolt, stood listening.

"Oh for heaven's sake," said Isabelle in disgust. "Open up! You've got the most insane ideas. Here, let me."

"No, I'll do it." Betty turned the bolt, eased open the door, looked through the crack. The corridor seemed clear.

Isabelle marched out. Betty shut and bolted the door. For a moment she stood listening at the door, but if there was any sound, the hiss of rain and swirl of water along the hull drowned it out.

She went back to bed, took up her book. It came to her presently that she had no idea what she was reading. She rubbed her eyes, started over.

No use. Her eyes drooped shut. She put the book down, closed her eyes while she waited for Isabelle.

Time passed. The area of her mind alert for Isabelle's return became impatient. She stirred, awoke, sat up, looked across at Isabelle's bed. There had been time enough for three or four showers. Perhaps she had stepped down the corridor to visit Mik Finsch.

Betty started to lean back, then froze. A soft sound in the corridor — Isabelle? Betty stared at the door. The bronze knob quivered, slowly twisted. Betty watched in fascination. The knob turned to its fullest extent. The door strained inward, pressed against the bolt.

The pressure relaxed, the knob slowly returned to its original position.

Five minutes passed. Betty got to her feet, went to the door on tiptoe, listened. No sound.

Presently she went back to her bed, lay down, cringing at the sound of the springs.

An hour passed. Where was Isabelle? With Finsch? Who had tried the door? If Isabelle were with Finsch, had someone else come to pay her a quiet visit? Who?

Betty awoke at two o'clock without realizing she had fallen asleep. The rain had stopped; the engines throbbed, incessant as a heart-beat, driving the *Garda* through the dark.

Betty wondered dully about Isabelle, then once again sank into slumber.

# 6

The morning sun awoke Betty. The sky was bright as a plate. She languidly sat up, threw her legs to the floor, surveyed Isabelle's empty bed. Strange.

Betty put on her robe, went to the door, stopped short, reluctantly turned away. Terrible when a person was afraid to go to the bathroom… She could wait.

She brushed her teeth, dressed, went to the door again. She put her hand to the bolt, hesitated. Suppose something massive and powerful pushed through to take her by surprise, to smother her outcry before she could voice it? Betty drew her hand away from the bolt.

For a moment she stood fidgeting, anxious to reach the bathroom, angry at her own fear. She heard cheerful Italian voices, footsteps. She snapped the bolt, marched out into the corridor.

Perhaps by coincidence, Mik Finsch stood outside the door to his own cabin, as if he had just emerged. He looked tired and haggard, the skin of his face hung loose. Their eyes met and there was an instant of complete communication. Betty followed the second mate and the second engineer down a deck, turned off and walked swiftly to the Catos' cabin. She knocked, anxiously watching over her shoulder. The door swung open, Ora looked out. "Good morning! I see you're still with us."

"I won't be unless I get to the bathroom. I don't dare go alone."

"Just a sec. I'll come stand outside the door."

"I know it's silly."

"Never mind that. Better silly than sorry."

On the way down to the mess-hall, Ora asked about Isabelle. "How did you two get along? More quarrels?"

"No," said Betty. "In fact she apologized. Then she went to take a shower and never came back. I suppose she spent the night with Finsch."

Ora grunted. "She cares very little what anyone thinks."

Betty felt a perverse urge to defend Isabelle. Last night, for the first time, she had found something likeable under the blonde and blue exterior. But she said nothing.

In the mess-hall Finsch sat alone at the back table. He looked up when Betty and Ora came, returned to his grapefruit. Isabelle must be dressing, thought Betty.

Breakfast passed and still no Isabelle. Harry Mayberry, now his usual self, made an inquiry. Betty shrugged. "I don't know where she is."

"She is ill?" asked the captain. "I send up the steward with coffee and orange juice."

"I don't know whether she's ill or not. She wasn't in the cabin. Maybe Mr. Finsch has seen her."

"I?" asked Finsch. "No. I have not seen her. Not since last night."

Betty stared at him. She turned to the captain. "Isabelle went to take a shower last night. She never came back."

The captain put down his coffee, jumped to his feet. "Come, we look."

Isabelle was not aboard the *Garda*.

Betty noticed that everyone seemed to look at her queerly, even the Catos.

# Chapter X

## 1

THE GARDA WAS SAILING close along a tall green coast, with Punta Guionos astern and Cabo Blanco ahead. The air was heavy with heat; furious oily fire ran along the slick planes of the water; the horizons shimmered in the glare.

The least uncomfortable place aboard was under the awning on the top deck, in the breeze generated by the motion of the ship. Here sat the passengers in their coolest clothes, watching the mountains and valleys of Costa Rica pass astern.

Immediately after Isabelle's disappearance had been verified, Finsch and the captain conferred in the captain's cabin, while Betty fidgeted in a deck-chair. "What on earth can they be talking about?" she demanded peevishly.

Alec and Ora sat to her right, and beyond Harry Mayberry and Nello.

"I could guess," said Alec shortly. Ora said nothing. Her mouth was pursed into a peculiar round shape, like a dry rosebud.

"It's fantastic," said Betty. "Isabelle certainly never went of her own free will. And why should anyone else do anything to her?"

"Exactly," said Alec dryly. "Finsch had nothing to gain."

Betty fell silent. No one else seemed disposed for conversation.

A few minutes later the room-steward approached and politely told Betty that the captain wished to speak to her. There was dead silence as Betty left; but almost before she had disappeared down the stairs she heard the dry sardonic sound of Ora's voice. Betty's ears burned in anger and humiliation. What had come over these people so suddenly?

The captain, looking angry and harassed, was sitting as before be-hind his table with Finsch in a small cane-bottomed chair to the left. In spite of the heat Finsch seemed like a man suffering from chill. His skin was dry and taut over his heavy bones; his eyes glittered like graphite; his half-grin had drawn back into a fox-like grimace.

The captain motioned Betty to a seat.

"We must discuss this terrible situation," intoned the captain. "There will be an investigation in Panama, but perhaps you may wish to say something now."

Betty sat straight up in the chair. Her voice cracked with indigna-tion. "Say something? About what?"

"Naturally, about Mrs. Calder's disappearance."

"I've told you everything I know. She left the cabin about half-past nine to take a shower. That's the last I saw of her."

"Did you quarrel?"

"Good heavens no! She told me she was sorry about the fight. We were quite friendly."

Finsch shook his head slightly, as if he found this hard to credit. Betty glared at him, then back at the captain. "I don't like the tone of your questions."

The captain showed no signs of softening; if anything his face be-came even sterner. "It is a terrible situation. Think of the publicity. There will be talk in the newspapers. The *Garda* of the Mediterranean Line, commanded by Captain Alberto Frascatore."

"It is not nice," said Finsch.

"It is more than not nice; it is terrible. I never have known a trip like this. Where, then, is Mrs. Calder?"

"I haven't the slightest idea. Ask Mr. Finsch."

Finsch held out his hands, raised his eyebrows, disclaiming all knowledge. "I do not know. Let us face facts. You accused me in the matter of Alan Calder. It is stupid, but —" he pursed his lips "— it is possible. Now Mrs. Isabelle Calder. It is stupid and also it is impos-sible. Of all the persons on this ship, she is the last I would harm. Now we will think back into the past. It is not nice but we must face facts. Miss Haverhill quarrels with Mr. Bunpole, because he follows her aboard. Mr. Bunpole disappears — a suicide. At La Libertad she takes my gun — no, please let me finish — and Mr. Alan Calder is shot. A suicide. Yesterday she quarrels with Isabelle Calder, and last night Isabelle Calder is gone. Is it not strange?"

Betty could barely hold herself on her seat for anger. "How dare you distort things like that! You know they're not true! You're a liar, and a murderer!"

"I? That is absolute nonsense!" Finsch's voice was loud and heavy, and rattled the glass in the captain's bookcases. "I am known in many places through the world, and no man has ever dared call me these names."

Betty spoke in a soft and casual voice. "They're true though, aren't they?"

"They are not true. It is foolishness. You must know that I would not harm Isabelle."

"That may be so," said Betty. "But you wish to harm me. And for your information, something occurred to me just now when you mentioned Alan Calder. I know something else that proves you shot him, and not me, as you'd like to make people believe. We'll be in Panama tomorrow, and you can sweat until then." She rose to her feet. "Also, Captain, will you have the lock on the ladies' bathroom fixed? Right now? I don't dare…" Betty's voice dwindled; she was looking at Finsch. Because now the mystery of Isabelle's disappearance was illuminated. Everything was crystal-clear. Finsch had made a tragic mistake, heart-achingly pathetic, irresistibly comic. Betty laughed shrilly, pointed at Finsch. "You're a liar and a murderer, and also, you're a fool!"

Finsch's teeth glittered; he leaned forward, then sat back. He turned to the captain. "I fear Miss Haverhill is not well. I would suggest —"

"No, no," said Betty. "Don't worry, I'm quite well. Quite well, thank you, and I intend to stay quite well. Until Panama. Then I think I'll get drunk." She went to the door.

"Where are you going?" asked the captain gruffly.

"To my room. Where I will lock the door. You see, I don't want to disappear between now and tomorrow too."

"She is not well," rumbled Finsch. "That explains everything."

The captain put his hands flat on the table in a signal of dismissal. "There will be an investigation in Panama. I will radio ahead now."

"Please don't forget the lock on the bathroom door, Captain!"

"No. I will not forget. I forget nothing."

Betty ran across the thwart-ship passage, into her cabin, locked the door. Poor Isabelle, who had paid dearly for the use of a red shower-cap!

Betty sat on the bed. The sequence of events was plain. First, everyone knew that Betty regularly took a shower before retiring. It had become an invariable part of her routine. Secondly, Finsch knew that Betty's shower-cap was red and Isabelle's was blue; Betty had met him several times in the corridor. Both Isabelle and Betty wore white terry-cloth bathrobes; both were of a size. Finsch, peering through a crack in his door, expecting Betty, had glimpsed Isabelle walking into the bathroom in Betty's red shower-cap. Previously he had put the lock out of repair. Slipping out of his room, probably barefoot, he went to the bathroom, opened the door, eased in. Isabelle, behind the shower-curtain, with the water rushing past her ears would have seen nothing and heard nothing. Then — two great hands coming around the curtain, seizing the slender throat, crushing it like a flower-stem. There would have been very little struggle, a few kicks, a feeble tearing at the hands, before the body sagged dead. At this moment, Finsch, pulling the shower-curtain aside, would learn his mistake. There would be a moment of horror, even for Finsch. But, willy-nilly, he must carry out his plans. First, look out into the corridor, and listen — then, with the body hanging over his arm, lope aft, out on the bridge deck. A pause to reconnoiter, then down the ladder to the boat deck. Here, another pause, then two quick steps across the deck to the shadow behind the lifeboats. Now — lower the white body, release. There would be a slight splash. The body would submerge, sprawling head over heels through the wake. Presently it would float, a pale shape in the dark water, while the *Garda* moved off through the night.

He meant it to be me, thought Betty. He had gone to his cabin, he had sat on his bed, rubbing his chin. Then he had come quietly to Cabin #2 and tried the door. It had been locked and he had gone away.

Now he sat somewhere, smoking a cigar and thinking. She had made a rash statement. She had told Finsch she could prove he had killed Alan Calder. Perhaps he knew what she meant. Twenty-four hours remained before Panama.

# 2

The heat in the cabin was stupefying. The sweat ran off her body, soaked the sheet. Betty became furiously angry. Why should she lie down here in the heat? She was guilty of nothing, absolutely nothing!

She rose to her feet, splashed cold water into her face, dried herself. Isabelle's underclothes, still in a heap on the deck, reproached her; she tucked them into the closet.

At the door she hesitated, then defiantly unbolted and flung it wide. She marched out into the empty corridor, went aft to the ladder, climbed to the top deck.

The entire complement of passengers sat along the rail, in three groups. Finsch and the two Germans lounged at the forward edge of the awning, behind a table supporting six empty and three half-empty beer-bottles. The Salvadorean couple sat in identical postures, short legs thrust out, chubby hands gripping the arms of the chair, staring cataleptically toward the passing shore. By the after rail sat Alec, Ora, Harry Mayberry and Nello, talking in desultory mutters. The conversation died when Betty came up behind them.

"Oh, hello," said Ora. Alec self-consciously pulled a chair forward. No one looked directly at Betty. The silence lengthened and became awkward. Incredible! thought Betty. How swiftly they had changed their faces. Resentment swelled up inside her like a gas. She looked along the line of faces: Alec, owlish and smug; Ora with her hair and her opinions, equally blatant; sleek nasty Harry Mayberry; arrogant Nello. There they sat, her erstwhile friends, anxious to avoid involvement, unwilling to meet her eye.

Betty studied them a moment, her lip curled in contempt. Secretly they enjoyed the excitement, so long as they could observe from a distance. Already they were framing stories to tell their friends! Damned if she'd let them enjoy her troubles! Damned if she'd fall in with their mealy-mouthed skittishness, pretending that nothing had happened and that all were the best of friends.

"Don't mind me," said Betty wickedly. "I'm just a murderess. Go ahead with what you were saying."

Harry Mayberry chortled nervously, Ora sucked in her breath.

"None of you appear surprised. But then you'd figured it out for yourselves."

Alec said shortly, "No one's figured out anything. We're perplexed."

Betty gave a bitter peal of laughter. "'Perplexed'! That's a good word."

Ora snorted and hitched herself forward. "We're perplexed and hor-rified."

Betty began to feel as much dislike for Ora as she had for Isabelle. "Let's pretend that Isabelle committed suicide. We managed for Ted Bunpole. Then we can play cards this afternoon."

Ora's eyes snapped. "I see no excuse for your attitude, unless it's plain hysteria."

Alec cleared his throat uncomfortably. "We're all a little on edge. The heat, the events…"

Betty laughed scornfully. "Do you know Finsch's theory? Whoever quarrels with me, disappears. So be careful."

"Not a pleasant subject for a joke," muttered Alec.

"Joke! Who's laughing?"

"Certainly not Isabelle," said Ora.

"Nor Ted," said Betty. "But you must be wondering why I shot Alan Calder." She looked along the line of faces. She had succeeded in embarrassing them, so much to the good. But there was also cautious interest in their glances.

"You really think I did this," said Betty softly. "Pushed Isabelle in the water."

"No, of course not," said Alec. "It's wildly improbable…" His voice dwindled away.

"Somebody is guilty," said Betty reasonably. "Isabelle never jumped overboard alone! And why should Finsch help her over?" From the corner of her eye she saw Finsch look up as the sound of his name reached him.

Alec brought out his pipe. "Naturally we all speculate. It's human nature to expect the unexpected. I refuse to form any opinions. I don't have enough facts."

Betty laughed sardonically. "I'll give you a fact. Last night Isabelle borrowed my red shower-cap. She wore a bathrobe exactly like mine."

There was a short silence.

Alec filled his pipe, lit it. "Hmf. That explains a great deal."

Ora said nothing, but Betty saw her steal a shocked glance toward Finsch, now emptying his third bottle of beer. Nello was puzzled, not fully comprehending. Harry Mayberry blew out his plump cheeks. "I see why you're upset. You're scared stiff."

Alec took the pipe from his mouth, looked at it intently. "Why don't you sleep with Ora tonight, and I'll take your cabin? You'll feel safer."

Ora turned her head quickly, looked from Alec to Betty, back to Alec.

"No, thank you," said Betty, to Ora's manifest relief. "There might be another mistake."

"No, no," protested Alec unconvincingly. "I'd be glad —"

Betty interrupted. "I'm safe, once my door is locked." She glanced past the Salvadorean couple, and the engineers. Finsch met her eye, gave her a slow companionable wink. Betty turned sharply away, a quiver of nausea in her stomach. "Why can't this damn ship go faster?" she said in a low harsh voice, strange to her own ears. "I've never been on anything I've hated so much…"

# 3

From habit rather than hunger the passengers went below for lunch. Betty nibbled at a piece of steak, ate an orange, drank a glass of wine. The captain sat with a set face, looking into his plate the entire meal, saying no word to anyone. Alec made one or two facetious attempts, each of which Ora squelched. Finsch ate alone at the table to the back, seemingly with his usual good appetite.

Betty left while Finsch was still busy with his fruit. She ran up to her cabin. The heat was as stupefying as ever; she took a book, went up on the top deck.

The deck was vacant except for herself. She glanced nervously toward the stairs…Ridiculous to be so alarmed! said part of her brain. Another said, not ridiculous at all, there's good reason for all possible caution, and more too! Because Mik Finsch must be growing ever more desperate. Yet he had eaten his lunch with composure! What was the source of Finsch's equanimity? Tomorrow the *Garda* arrived at Panama, and the ship would swarm with police. Evidently Finsch planned to kill her tonight. Betty's heart began to beat furiously. Fantastic but real!

Up the stairs came the familiar broad-brimmed hat, the complacent head with the cigar. Betty's heart, already beating fast, gave a great pound. Finsch looked placidly here and there like a realtor appraising a piece of property. He nodded courteously to Betty, who stood watching with every muscle taut.

Finsch took off his hat, fanned himself once or twice, started to stroll toward Betty.

Betty promptly turned and walked to the steps leading down to the wheel-house. Here she paused watchfully. Finsch shrugged, went to the port rail, sank luxuriously into a deck-chair. Betty moved back into the shade, and sat where she could watch Finsch's every move. He paid no attention to her.

Alec and Ora came up on deck, took the seats they had occupied before lunch. Betty crossed the deck, joined them.

Abeam of the ship was a long heavy finger of land pointing out into the sea. "Punta Burica," said Alec. "Half Costa Rica, half Panama. We are about to cross the Gulf of Chiriqui, and will see no more land until just before we make the canal. We pass the Peninsula de Azuero in the night, thereupon turning almost due north. This navigational lore I have just acquired in the chart room. I had to spill it before I forgot it."

Betty sat rigidly, staring over the water, now pure tropical blue, transparent and luminous. She stirred uneasily, finally leaned forward, whispered to Ora, who nodded. "Don't worry. I'll keep my eye on him."

Betty gratefully went below.

# 4

The bathroom lock had been repaired; feeling relatively secure with Ora on guard, Betty showered, changed her clothes, returned to the top deck with a book.

The afternoon dragged past. At four o'clock she went below with the Catos for tea, and played solitaire for almost an hour. Nello thought to engage her in conversation, but Betty ignored him and Nello presently departed. After this morning, she could never again whole-heartedly like her fellow passengers. How could they think such ugly things of her? They must know — but perhaps she expected too much. They were only acquaintances; she had no claim upon their loyalty.

Betty sighed, shuffled the cards, dealt a new set-up. In two weeks she had done a great deal of growing up. The smart young Betty Haverhill who had boarded the *Garda* was a person already vague in outline. Why must experience always be disillusioning? Why could not ideals be confirmed instead of exploded? This systematic puncturing of bright dreams — was this the meaning of maturity?

The mess-boy came in to set the tables and Betty put away the cards. She had failed to unveil the ultimate meaning of life; still, she no longer hated Alec, Ora, Harry and Nello. Mik Finsch was another matter. One might hate Mik Finsch without reserve. All day he had sat placid, almost somnolent. What was in his mind, what was he planning? Her imagination created a set of images so macabre that she winced and made a soft troubled sound. The mess-boy glanced at her from the corner of his eye.

Betty jumped up, went to the door, looked along the corridor. No one in sight. She took a firm grip on her courage, went swiftly to the stairs, climbed to the bridge deck, walked to the captain's cabin, shying like a nervous horse as she passed Finsch's door.

From inside the captain's cabin came the sound of voices, which broke off as she knocked. The door opened, the chief steward looked out.

"I want to talk to the captain," said Betty.

"Come!" called the captain.

Betty entered. A bottle of vermouth stood on the table with three glasses; the captain, with the chief steward and chief engineer, was enjoying an aperitif before dinner. The captain's face, rubicund and jovial, with the big nose pinker than usual, changed quickly at the sight of Betty.

"Ah, Miss Haverhill," said the captain courteously. "Sit down. Maybe you like a glass of vermouth?"

"Thank you." Betty accepted the glass because it seemed easier than refusing.

There was a silence. Betty sipped the vermouth, with the eyes of all three men focused on her. The captain waited stonily. He's making it as hard for me as possible, thought Betty; he knows perfectly well what I want to talk about.

The chief steward rose to his feet, spoke to the captain; the chief engineer followed suit. But the captain waved them back into their seats, speaking tersely in Italian.

Betty suppressed her indignation and anger. The captain looked at her expectantly. "Well, Miss Haverhill, you have something to tell me, maybe?"

His tone was somehow false, almost sly; Betty, in a flash of comprehension, understood everything. He thinks I've come here to confess! She gripped the glass until her knuckles shone white, resisting an impulse to throw the vermouth into the watchful face.

"No," she said harshly. "I don't have anything to tell you."

"Then why do you come?"

"Because I'm afraid. I want some kind of protection!"

The captain leaned back in his chair, thrusting his lips out judiciously. "I thought you had come to tell me something. Why are you afraid?"

"I'm afraid of dying, naturally!" snapped Betty. "I'm afraid of Finsch!"

"Ah ha ha! Mr. Finsch has threatened you?"

Betty stared at him in wonder and wrath. "For heaven's sake, Captain, please don't be more stupid than necessary. You know perfectly well what Finsch has done; he killed —"

"Just one moment, Miss Haverhill! I am stupid, I am only Captain Frascatore. But I am wise enough to accuse no one. It is very dangerous thing to accuse without proof."

"But I have proof!"

"Bah! That is no proof. I have looked. I asked Mr. Finsch. He laughs. He says, 'How does this girl get these papers? It is strange.' I say, 'Yes, it is strange.'"

"But —"

"Just one moment. I do not accuse. I say nothing. But I know Mr. Finsch. He is very sensible, he is not an hysterical young girl. Why should he do crazy things? There is no reason. Mr. Ted Bunpole? No reason. Mr. Alan Calder? No reason. Mrs. Isabelle Calder? No reason. It is ridiculous!"

"Ridiculous or not," cried Betty, "he did it! He's a megalomaniac, a complete egotist."

The captain shrugged. "I do not know these words. I do not understand."

"It's not the words; you don't understand human nature! If—"

"Hah!" exclaimed the captain, his gold teeth glinting in the sourest of all grins. "It is you, the young girl, who understands, and I, Captain Frascatore, am the stupid one. Very well, that is what you think. But sometimes I am not so stupid! I know of the child delinquents. I know that—"

"Will you please listen to me?"

"Very well, I listen." The captain folded his arms, leaned back, impassive and magisterial. "What is that you want?"

"I want some kind of assurance that I'll be safe!"

The captain nodded. "That is reasonable. I will give you the assurance. Are you in danger now?"

"No, of course not."

"Are you in danger in the mess-hall?"

"No."

"Are you in danger in your cabin?"

"With the door locked, no. But—"

"Where are you in danger?"

"I don't know! I wish—"

The captain rose to his feet. "Come. I will take you to your cabin. You may lock the door. For dinner I will come. We will go down together. After dinner I will take you to your cabin, and you may lock the door once more. I give you the assurance."

Blind with rage and frustration, Betty jumped to her feet, ran out into the passage. Behind her the voices started again. The captain's short sharp bark of laughter followed her along the passage.

# 5

Betty sat in her cabin until dinner time, and opened her door then only when she heard voices in the corridor.

Finsch was already in his place when she arrived, bending studiously over his soup. Betty passed him with a shrinking of her flesh, slipped into her seat, beside Alec.

There was little conversation during the meal. Betty ate half a plate of soup, toyed with a bit of fish, drank half a glass of wine, every nerve aware of the man sitting eight feet behind her back. She could hear the scrape of his knife and fork, the squeak of his chair, the sound of his chewing. She felt his own awareness of her, his absorption in the problem which faced him, and what small appetite she had left fled.

She waited for the Catos and left the mess-hall close on their heels. They climbed to the top deck and came out into a blaze of ruddy light from a glorious red and gold sunset. Clouds streamed forty miles across the sky; the ocean glittered with color. For an instant Betty seemed to apprehend the flaming message: hope and the tragedy of hope, the ultimate victories still far in the future, a golden emotion beyond the reach of words. The sunset faded; color was conquered by the gray dusk, the golden message was lost.

Twilight veiled the ocean. There was no land to be seen, and the *Garda*, moving across the dim expanse, was the single reality of the universe.

Time passed. There was subdued talk and guarded speculation. At half-past ten the Catos stretched and yawned and spoke of bed. Betty would willingly have sat up all night, but only Nello rose to her hint, and Betty said no, she thought she'd go to bed too. Alec went with her to her cabin. They inspected the door, the lock, the hinges, then checked under the beds and in the closets.

"Everything seems secure," said Alec. "You'll probably spend the quietest night of your life."

"And the most wide-awake too."

"Well, goodnight," said Alec. He paused in the doorway. "Unless — er — do you want to…er, ah…while I'm waiting?"

"It's probably a wise idea."

Alec waited till she returned. "All clear?"

"Apparently," said Betty, making a wan attempt to smile. "If not…"

"Just yell. But don't worry. You'll be perfectly safe."

"I suppose so." Betty looked at him wistfully, wishing that, in spite of Ora's disapproval, she had traded beds for the night. "Goodnight, Alec."

"Goodnight."

The door closed. Betty threw the bolt, pulled at the knob; the door was secure.

She undressed down to her briefs: it was too hot for pajamas. She lay down on the bed, and tried to read. But the book served only as something solid on which to rest her hands. How could she think of anything but herself and Finsch and Panama? And of the other faces she had looked at and spoken to: Ted Bunpole, Alan Calder, Isabelle, all now far away and gone. She shivered, put the book aside. What a nightmare, this trip!

Betty sat up in bed. A *rap rap rap* on the door.

She got to her feet, walked slowly across the room. There was another knock; the door-knob turned, the door rattled.

"Who's there?" called Betty.

"It is I, Captain Frascatore. Do not open. I am making a check. You are all right?"

"Yes."

"Then you are safe?"

"So far."

"Very well. Do not open the door, and you will have nothing to fear."

"I don't intend to open the door."

"Good. Sleep well."

Betty went back to bed. She turned off the light, but almost at once switched it on again…What in the world was Finsch up to? Certainly not sleep. His brain must be fermenting with the need to kill her… But how? Suppose she were under the same compulsion, what means would she use to kill someone locked in a cabin? First, entice the victim out. Betty smiled grimly. Finsch would entice in vain. He must realize this, and this was his problem. He could not lure her out; he could not get in. But still he must kill her. He could not shoot her through the porthole; there was nowhere for him to stand, even if he owned another gun. He could not poison her — or could he? Betty decided not to brush her teeth, which tonight she had neglected in any case. He might have loaded the tooth-paste with cyanide. There might be a booby-trap in the medicine closet, a time-bomb in the suitcase…Boomerangs, bolos, black widow spiders — her imagination was running away with her…

Betty dozed, snapping awake at every sound: a distant voice, footsteps in the corridor.

The ship gradually became quiet, until nothing could be heard but the beat of the engines, the passage of the water along the hull, a soft all-pervading hum from the dynamo and air-blowers.

At half-past eleven she switched off the light once more, and lay sweating in the dark. The sheet felt like wet newspaper, the pillow was lumpy and smelled sour.

Twelve o'clock: a stir as the watches changed, a brief opening and closing of doors. At ten minutes after twelve the ship was quiet again.

Now was the dangerous time, when the life of the ship reached its lowest ebb...Quarter after twelve, twenty, twenty-five after, twelve-thirty. Betty lay waiting, staring into the dark.

Now. She felt a thrill of anticipation. A slight noise from somewhere. The deck above? A faint scraping sound. Betty turned on the light. The handle which controlled the ceiling ventilator was rotating; the ventilator was being twisted open from above. She stared. What was he trying to do? She jumped up, seized the handle, twisted to close the ventilator. From overhead came a rattle, a clank. Something hissing like a snake fell toward her head. She jumped back. It struck the deck, burst with a powerful dull sound. Clouds of fume sprang forth, Betty jumped away.

She took a breath: acrid gas caught at her throat. Her eyes began to smart, to water. Tear-gas. Finsch's tear-gas. She opened her mouth to yell, and drew in her breath. Her throat seemed to run with acid, and she made only a hoarse croaking sound. Air, air! She was smothering! So this was Finsch's plan! He would drive her from the cabin. But no. Not while she had her wits about her. The porthole. She could find fresh air at the porthole, she could scream for help. She clawed her way across Isabelle's bed, sobbing, weeping, eyes full of pain. The porthole showed as a black disk into nothingness. She pushed her head out, in instant reflex snatched it back. Barely in time. A rope looped underneath snapped up. It would have caught under her throat, pulling the back of her neck against the upper edge of the porthole. A heave from above — death. But the rope caught only the point of her chin, banging her head back against the porthole cover, then rolled loose, scraping her chin. She fell back on the bed, rolled over, hitting her head against the closet.

She had to breathe. She gasped but the gas was worse than nothing; it ate like fire. Betty's mind worked sluggishly. She would strangle without air; Finsch waited at the porthole with his noose. She would run to the door, throw it open, call for help. He would know this; he would be racing down the steps. She must hurry; there were only seconds.

She picked herself up, and unmindful of her near-nudity staggered to the door. She fumbled for the bolt; where was it? She snapped it back. Now, fling open the door! Breathe! Scream! Run!

The door opened; she tottered out. There was Finsch, barefoot, in his shorts, coming down the corridor like a fabulous monster — a smooth-skinned gorilla, a naked bear. His eyes glistened, his teeth showed in a great grin. Betty tried to scream; her voice caught in her throat, her knees sagged under her. He was on her; his hands found her throat, there was a loud hiss in her brain, she went limp.

Without pausing he slung her over his arm, ran back along the corridor. There had been no sound, nothing except the gasp, the shuffle of feet. No one saw, no one knew. Out into the dark, down the steps to the boat deck. A pause — only a second. Finsch was in great haste. He sprang across the deck, took shelter behind the life-boats, thrust the limp white form over the side, let go. At the last instant she recovered sufficient awareness to grasp, to reach. Her fingers found the edge of the deck. She hung on, swinging against the rough black hull, with the black water hissing below. Finsch reached down, worked at the frail fingers. She dropped, tumbling over, and struck the rushing water on her back.

She came to the surface, gasped for air, tried to scream. A wave hit her in the mouth, she choked. The dark hull slid past. She spat out the water, called, but all that came was a plaintive croak. There was a rumbling in her ears: the propellers. She was caught up, swept into the boil, churned an incalculable distance down into darkness, and through no particular effort of her own, up and out into the air.

She took a deep shuddering gasp of air, and now she screamed. It sounded like the call of a sea-bird, wandering the ocean by night. She saw the stern of the *Garda*, a black squat shape above the luminous boil of the wake. It rose and fell, and became smaller. The stern-light looked back at her.

The wake smoothed out, the boil subsided. The *Garda* was low and dark; the stern-light was far away.

Betty called and called, until her voice grew faint. There was no more sound of propeller; the stern-light was only a speck. Betty looked after the ship, with tears of sadness streaming from her eyes. It was so terribly lonely here in the dark, in the dark ocean, with the black sky above, and her only link with life the distant wink of the stern-light. And then she could see it no more, and she was altogether alone. There was a faint sigh of wind, of water rising and falling, but nothing more.

# 6

Finsch stood behind the life-boats, breathing heavily. He looked, listened. No sound, no stir. The wing of the bridge showed a vacant rectangle of sky under the flying bridge: the mate and the look-out were on the other side of the ship. With great agility Finsch sprang across the vacant space, mounted the ladder to the bridge deck. He glanced down the corridor: empty. The ship was asleep. Such small noise that had occurred, the hoarse breathing, the pad of bare feet, the door opening — they had not been heard. There was an acrid reek in the passage which soon would dissipate.

Finsch went to Cabin #2, stepped in, shut the door. He carefully picked up the fragments of the gas-grenade, tucked them in his pocket, almost with affection: they had served him well. He smoothed the bed, erasing the appearance of disorder. Then he took a facial tissue from its box, opened the drawer to the desk, and with his fingers protected, took out a ball-point pen and a piece of paper. With one or two precursory flourishes he printed in neat round letters:

*I am sorry. Betty.*

He looked at the message, shook his head. It was not good. With more time at his disposal he could do better — but this must suffice.

He propped the note on the pillow, looked about the room. The book: he picked it up, closed it, laid it on the shelf.

He saw the purse, opened it, examined the wallet, considered the money, hesitated, replaced the wallet. There was nothing else of interest, except the driver's license. He compared the signature with his printed note, nodded. Better than he had hoped. He made a last inspection of the room, went to the door, listened. No sound. Using a corner of the towel, he opened the door a crack, listened, looked, then stepped out into the passage, closed the door gently, and strolled to his own cabin.

A few minutes later he was back. Again, the quick look up and down the passage, the opening of the door. From his pocket he took a bright red shower-cap. He tossed it into the wash-basin. Smiling, he returned to his own cabin, laid himself on his bed. He heaved a great sigh of satisfaction, and slept.

# CHAPTER XI

## 1

THE *GARDA* WAS GONE; the stern-light had dwindled and vanished. The realities were two: the dark sky full of stars, the black gulf below. There was also herself, her consciousness, the ghostly movement of her arms and legs; but these were only half-real...She stretched, floated, rising and falling in complete relaxation. Uncertainties were behind her; she had come past the boundary of fear. She was part of the awful grandeur, the same stuff as the cosmos. It was calm and very peaceful, and she knew that if she dared open her mind, a terrible exaltation would come upon her...Nonetheless, a sad and desolate business to sink from sight out here in the lonely wastes. Finsch had triumphed; he had forced her from her retreat, he had dropped her contemptuously into darkness. Now he sailed grandly away on the warm ship; she was defeated and left behind. Finsch: the emotion was enormous; too large for feeling.

She turned over, floated on her back. Never had the night seemed so beautiful. The stars shone clear and soft and white. There was the North Star. Land would lie to the north-east, at an unknown distance. Land? She wondered idly. At sunset only ocean could be seen; they had been crossing a gulf or indentation into the coast of Panama. She looked to the north-east but could see only darkness. She listened: there was nothing but the sound of waves and wind.

She started to swim, an overhand side-stroke which she had always found efficient. Land could not be too far distant. She could swim — how fast? A mile an hour? Perhaps. How long could she swim? Hard to say. She was by no means a trained athlete, but she was healthy and strong...

Land! The thought fired her. What of sharks? So far she had refused to consider them. The darkness suddenly seemed more friendly. It would hide her from the sharks... She swam rather faster. But there was no help for it. If they got her, they got her.

She watched Polaris, the North Star. The coast of Panama in this area ran almost east to west; north-east was the direction to swim. If only she knew the distance to shore! And what of the currents? Perhaps they swept her to sea as fast as she swam toward land... Speculation was useless. Her courses of action had been reduced to a minimum. She could either sink or swim. She swam. She became tired; she rested. But now when she rested, she thought of the depths below, the great hole out of which only the air in her lungs supported her, and she was stimulated to swim more steadily than her muscles enjoyed.

Time passed. She swam more slowly, with an ache in her shoulders and dull pain in the palms of her hands. These meant nothing; she ignored them. Slow, steady: a mile an hour. She took to counting her strokes; one hundred, then rest. Another hundred on the other side, then rest. Then a hundred breast-strokes. She did not dare swim a crawl; the splash of her feet might attract attention.

A hundred strokes, rest. A hundred strokes, rest. Time: minutes, hours. Stars dipped out of sight, new stars appeared. The wind rose, blew lustily for a few minutes, then stopped dead.

She swam, now tired to the point of exhaustion. Her arms and legs moved with great effort; she was swimming much more slowly.

Overhead, a low cloud blotted out the sky. There was a patter of rain. The stars were obscured; how could she find her way? The rain increased, there was the flash of lightning, the rumble of thunder. She thought, I'm tired! But I can't stop. Because if I stop, I'll go to sleep. If I go to sleep, I'll drown.

The rain refreshed her, but all too quickly ceased. The lightning persisted. She noticed something, her heart stood still. She waited and watched till the next lightning flash: yes, there it was! The dark loom of a mountain, low and dishearteningly far away.

Almost at the same instant she saw a light, much nearer, not half a mile distant. It seemed to be a small boat, with a single man in it. A fisherman. She swam anxiously toward the light, putting every ounce of energy into her strokes. Even so, her progress seemed dreadfully slow. Suppose he started his motor and moved on before she reached him? It would be more than she could bear.

Side-stroke, breast-stroke: no count, no resting. Her arms and legs hurt, the palms of her hands felt as if they were bruised.

The fisherman never moved except to dip with his net into the glow cast by his light. She could see him clearly, a short thin dark-skinned man wearing a blue shirt and ragged tan trousers.

Close now. A hundred yards, fifty yards — a hundred feet, fifty feet. But she was safe, safe! She started to sob with relief. "Hello," she called. "Hello, señor. I'm over here in the water."

The fisherman raised his head, stood up in the boat, stared toward her, as she swam into the outer limits of illumination. "Don't be alarmed," she called cheerfully, "I fell from a ship."

The man's eyes seemed to start from his head; he went the color of paste. He shouted a hoarse anguished cry, sprang to his outboard motor. "No, don't worry!" she called. "I'm human, I've been swimming for hours; please take me aboard your boat."

The motor refused to catch, the man's fingers trembled on the rope. She swam closer — thirty feet, twenty feet. The man's face was the picture of horror; he seized an oar, struck at her. Again he picked up his starting rope, wound, pulled. The motor caught, the boat lurched ahead.

"Don't go," she called. "Please don't go. I'm so tired. Please take me with you."

But the fisherman, bending low, paid no heed. The boat scuttled away like a cockroach, fast as the outboard motor could push it. She called after him, sobbing: "Please come back, please don't leave me."

The sound of the motor came across the water a long time, but finally she could hear it no more. And now the dark ocean seemed more silent than ever.

She lay floating a long time, tears streaming from her eyes. She had abandoned hope and her desire for life, she had resigned herself to death — until she had seen the boat. Then the longing had struck her, life had never seemed more sweet... She felt dreary and dreadfully tired. Her arms hung from her shoulders like logs; her legs ached. Perhaps here, at this point, she would let herself drown; it was easier to drown than to live.

She composed herself, tried to sleep, in order to drown more pleasantly. The water ran back up her nose, causing her to cough…She would try to swim on. There was land somewhere near. The lightning had stopped, the stars were out again, all but the Big Dipper: it seemed to be lost. In that case, she must swim away from the stars she could see, toward the blank spot in the darkness.

A hundred weary strokes, rest. A hundred weary strokes, rest. Her mind wandered; she felt dazed. Her arms and legs went of themselves, without her volition or direction. She had merely come along to watch. An early morning swim. Because now it was morning, with a faint lemonade glow in the east. There were the mountains: she noticed them suddenly. The shore was not so far away after all. She could sense the line of surf, and thought she could hear it.

She made her weary limbs beat the water. A hundred strokes, rest. A hundred slow flaccid strokes, rest. She seemed only to paw at the water, passing her hands through it.

Dawn brightened the sky, the water became gray and heavy-looking. With visibility came the fear she had restrained during darkness: sharks. The shore was hardly a mile distant; the current seemed to be helping her as much as her swimming. Sharks. Dreadful things. Her foot kicked against something firm, something large and resilient. Her heart froze, she clenched her jaws to scream, but water splashed into her mouth, half-strangling her. She forgot about exhaustion, she forgot the pain of arms and legs. She arched on her stomach, flattened on top of the waves. She swam as powerfully as she could, eyes fixed on the shore, looking neither left nor right.

The beach sloped up into masses of dense dark vegetation. Behind rose low mountains, shaggy with trees. She stared at the beach: it hypnotized her; nothing else in the world existed. The sharks. Deep inside herself she laughed. They were afraid of her. She had died and still she lived. She was master of the sharks; they swam beside her as respectful escorts. Fear, restraint — words without meaning. She had triumphed over death, nothing was impossible to her. She was as old as life, as wise as the mountains, as remote from good and evil as rain…The surf tumbled her up on the shore, and she lay shuddering on the sand. Another surge moved her, carried her back, as if the sea loved her and only reluctantly would let her go. She felt for the ground, crawled up out of the water, lay quiet where beach and wave met. The sun rose red and cold: daylight played on her tired naked body.

# 2

She crawled past the wash-line and fell into the fine sand, her arms and legs limp as string. The sand felt wonderfully comfortable; she would have slept except for her mood, which was bliss. She scratched the sand with her water-wrinkled fingers, revelling in the silky grit. In all my life, she thought, I've never known such happiness. I've gained nothing; I have only what I had before. Why did I not feel joy then? I took life and living for granted: what could be more wasteful? Now that I've passed through death, I know the ecstasy of existence. Every instant of aware-ness is miraculous joy, every sensation is delight! Never again will I feel bored or dull. I need only remember lying on this beach, and instantly I'll be happy. And all the rest of my life I'll pity people who exist with-out joy. I'm lucky! I'm almost grateful to Mik Finsch!

Finsch: she thought of Finsch and she thought of the *Garda*. Twist-ing languidly over, sitting up, she looked across the surf, imagining the way she must have come. Presently she rose to her feet, and stood — swaying at first, then with greater steadiness. There was nothing to be gained reclining on the beach — especially when she wanted to reach Panama. She laughed aloud, her voice hoarse. This was pure joy. Mik Finsch would be surprised.

There were problems. She brushed the sand from her flanks. Clothes. She'd need covering more efficient than her nylon briefs. Perhaps she'd find something along the beach; if not she'd hold leaves in front of her-self... A minor matter. She was alive, she lived! Stretching her arms proudly, she looked over the sea. Venus emerging from the waves... Lord, I'm tired! But I don't want to sleep. I'm hungry, but I don't want to eat.

She started down the beach into the rising sun. I feel like a nymph, she thought — naked, unrestrained. The air, still cool, played on her skin; the sand felt pleasantly harsh on her feet.

The beach stretched ahead for half a mile, then was broken by a spur of rock protruding into the ocean. To her left, back from the beach, rose a wall of apparently virgin jungle, with low hills looming beyond.

Halfway to the rock the jungle gave way to a grove of banana plants. A banana would taste very good, thought Betty. She gingerly climbed the slope of the beach, hesitated at the verge of the cultivated ground, which was partly overgrown with harsh grass and dark-green morning-glory. There might well be snakes hiding under the growth. Or tarantulas. She spied a stalk with yellow fruit only a few yards away. Carefully she picked her way through the grass, reached toward the stalk. An enormous black wasp buzzed past her ear, settled on the banana she was about to pick. It walked back and forth, wings glistening, thorax twitching. Betty froze, hardly daring to move. The sloe-black eyes looked at her from a distance of not more than two feet.

"Excuse me," whispered Betty, and backed away. From a respectful distance she waited. Presently the wasp flew away. Betty picked four bananas, broke off two fronds, and returned to the beach. She ate the bananas and continued on her way, carrying the fronds. Now, if she met someone, she at least could cover herself, no matter how coyly.

At the end of the beach, she found a ruined hut from which she salvaged a piece of rotten coffee-sack. She took it down into the surf, rinsed out the dirt and bugs, carefully unravelled some of the threads, and by dint of careful tearing and tying, managed to make a precarious breech-clout, and a barely adequate halter.

There, said Betty to herself, it's unconventional but at least I'm decent.

A hint of a path led up from the beach. Keeping a wary eye open for snakes, dancing and limping over sharp edges, she climbed over the rock. At the crest she paused. Ahead lay another beach, curving sharply around to the left. Almost below wisps of smoke rose from three huts.

Betty descended as quickly as possible. In the first hut she found a white-haired old man with skin the color of tobacco and blind white eyes, a fat middle-aged woman in a dirty black dress, two big-eyed girls in flour-sack smocks.

"*Buenos dias,*" said Betty hopefully. "Does anyone here speak English?"

The woman made an astounded appraisal of Betty and her improvised garments.

"I want to go to Panama," explained Betty. "Panama City. I pay *mucho dinero.*"

The woman bustled forward out of her hut, making excited motions. Unable to decide whether the woman were antagonistic or merely agitated, Betty backed cautiously away.

The woman looked up and down the beach, asked a sharp question.

"I came in a boat," said Betty. She pointed to the ocean. "I swim." She made swimming motions. "I want to go to Panama City!"

The woman wheeled, called the two small girls. She instructed them in a brief volley of syllables, made a sweeping motion with her hand, and removed herself from any further connection with the affair.

The girls timidly started away, looking over their shoulders at Betty. Apparently it was intended that she follow them.

They took her a hundred yards down the beach, then turned under the trees along a rutted track of damp red clay sparkling with bits of white quartz. At one time the path had been used by carts, but now plants reached into the open space, groping for sunlight.

Wary of snakes, centipedes, tarantulas, scorpions and pincer beetles, Betty picked her way along the path. The two little girls stared over their shoulders at her from twenty feet ahead, sometimes walking backwards. As they seemed careless of where they put their feet, Betty took confidence and began to enjoy the walk through the jungle.

The path wound through a patch of bamboo, abruptly came out on a bluff of raw red earth overlooking a black-green river. A few yards toward the ocean was a village: several shops, a small stone church, two score huts of various sizes and conditions.

The girls took Betty to the church, ran off, presently returned with a bearded young priest in a rusty cassock. To Betty's intense pleasure he spoke English.

# 3

The village was named Morales; it was situated halfway along the Peninsula de Azuero, near that headland known as Morro de Puercos. The supply boat which touched at Morales three times a month was due in another week. There were no roads, no public transportation, no boats large enough to take her to the Canal Zone.

Betty said forlornly, "I'll be stuck here a week. I simply *must* get to the canal."

"I am sorry," said the priest. He smote his shaven pate, already glistening in the early morning heat. "Come. Perhaps you are in luck!"

He started to lead her from the church, then reconsidered. "Wait here, if you will." Presently he returned with a dress and a pair of straw sandals.

"Oh wonderful!" Betty exclaimed. "You've no idea how this sack itches."

"I know," said the priest sadly. "Sometimes I must wear it myself."

The dress was black with a magenta flounce; it fit Betty much too tightly and smelled of camphor; nevertheless she wore it with great relief.

The priest conducted her to a dock along the river-bank. After mild argument, a young Indian, naked except for faded shorts, brought a skiff fitted with an outboard motor alongside, and they embarked.

They rode up the black-green river for half an hour. Sometimes the stream flowed among low islands covered with bright green plants and red flowers; sometimes under a shoulder of the red basaltic earth, with vegetation hanging over them in festoons.

There was no sound but the growl of the motor. The water ahead lay smooth as glass, covered with a silky skin. Several times the priest pointed out alligators, and Betty saw a beautiful white crane flapping slowly on soft wings.

They entered a region where the trees rose along the shore to a tremendous height, and presently the river broadened into a lake. The boat headed toward a group of buildings and open sheds roofed with corrugated aluminum. Under one of the sheds was a bright yellow bulldozer, red-faced drums of fuel and a jeep. A boat-house projected into the lake; underneath floated a small hydroplane. A sign over the main office read:

HAWORTH AND COMPANY
HARDWOODS

"Now we will see," said the priest. "If we are in luck Lionel will be in the office."

Lionel was a thin young man with a pugnacious snub-nosed face, stiff straw-colored hair. "Well, well, well," he said. "What have we here? You are welcome. To say I am surprised is an understatement."

"I am surprised to be here too," said Betty.

"Come in, please." Lionel led them through the door into the office, which was screened on all four sides. "Can I offer you a coke?"

Betty and the priest accepted; Lionel took three cans from the refrigerator, opened them. "This young lady fell off a ship last night," said the priest. "She swam ashore and wants to reach Panama."

Lionel grimaced. "You fell overboard?"

"I was dropped overboard," said Betty.

"You don't seem particularly the worse for it."

"I'm not. I'm so glad to be alive, I'll never be sad or angry or cross again."

"Exactly the kind of girl I'm looking for," said Lionel. "Who pushed you in? Husband? Boy friend?"

"No. Just a man."

"I see. Presumably you want to have the law on him."

"Yes. I don't hate him any more — not very much — but I want to see the look on his face when I show up in dry clothes."

Lionel looked at the electric clock. "I'll fly you in on one — no, two conditions."

"Anything," said Betty. "Absolutely anything — so long as it doesn't include swimming."

"No, no swimming. First, I want to come with you, to see the man's face. Second, I want to take you to dinner tonight."

Betty nodded. "I agree."

"Then let's go. What time does your ship dock?"

"About eleven."

"We'll be too late to meet it. But we'll be close behind."

"Er — can I borrow some money from you? I want to pay for the boat and this dress."

"I'll take care of it. You can settle with me later."

While Lionel was easing the hydroplane out from under the shelter Betty asked rather guiltily, "You won't get into trouble taking me in like this? Won't your boss be upset?"

Lionel pointed toward the sign HAWORTH HARDWOODS. "My name happens to be Lionel Haworth, which allows me a certain degree of freedom."

"Are you Haworth and Company in person?"

"Oh no. Uncle Ed is Haworth. I'm a minor part of the company. This is Camp Number Six. But don't worry about the plane. I have to fly in tomorrow anyway."

They climbed into the cabin; Betty waved goodbye to the priest who stood watching rather wistfully.

The motor clicked over, caught, roared, idled; the hydroplane drifted over the lake. At the far end it swung about; the motor roared in earnest, the plane skimmed over the water, rose over the trees, flew into the east.

The priest sighed, got into the skiff.

The outboard motor started, a weak simulation of the plane. The boat departed. The clearing was in silence, except for bird calls, and off in the forest the faint sound of power saws and presently the fall of a tree.

# Chapter XII

1

THE *GARDA* SWUNG AT ANCHOR outside the mouth of the canal, among half a dozen ships of as many different flags: Norwegian, Japanese, Liberian, British, German, Dutch — all, except the *Garda*, waiting for a canal pilot and clearance. Transit of the *Garda* had been delayed pending completion of police inquiries, already in progress.

Betty and Lionel Haworth rode out in an official launch, escorted by a plain-clothes man from the United States Marshal's office. The *Garda* looked as familiar as Betty's own home. There — the porthole to her cabin; there — she suddenly shivered, put her face in her hands.

"Here," said Lionel, "what's the trouble?"

Betty vainly tried to control her voice. "I don't know if I can face the man. I'll probably faint, or do something ridiculous."

"He must be an interesting chap."

"Yes. This has been an interesting trip."

They drove underneath the long black hull, circled toward the embarkation ladder.

"I'll be glad when this is over," Betty muttered. "I feel embarrassed — as if I were doing something rude…"

Lionel laughed uneasily. "You're a strange one. If it were me —" he reflected. "Anyway, it won't take long. Or rather, it may take long, but it's got to be done."

"I suppose."

The launch halted, the two jumped across to the landing, followed by the plain-clothes man. The seaman on gangway watch stared in

— 164 —

astonishment. The plain-clothes man spoke to him. "Take us to the captain, sonny. Understand? *El Capitano!*"

Looking slack-jawed over his shoulder at Betty, the seaman led them into the ship.

Back again! The dim corridors, the bustle in the galley, the smells and sounds at once so familiar and so repellent!

They climbed the familiar stairs to the bridge deck, went around to the captain's cabin. The plain-clothes man knocked. The door was opened by a tall lean man in a light blue suit.

"Hello, Hank. Who've you got here?"

"One of your principals: Miss Haverhill, Lieutenant Colby."

"Haverhill?" Betty was conscious of keen startled eyes. "Miss Betty Haverhill?"

"Yes. I've got quite a lot to tell you."

"Please come in."

They entered the captain's cabin. Captain Frascatore sat crouched over the table wearing a harassed frown. He saw Betty; his jaw sagged. He leaned forward, pointed a trembling hand. "It is she — this is the woman!"

Betty stepped slowly forward. "I am what woman?"

"You are Betty Haverhill! What are you doing here?"

# 2

Betty told her story. The captain sat with a stony face, staring at his hands. Lieutenant Colby, the plain-clothes man and Lionel Haworth listened with sympathy.

"You've certainly been through a terrible experience," said the lieutenant.

"Just one moment," said the captain harshly. "I accuse no one, of course, but we must remember that there is still no proof. We are obliged to be cautious."

"Captain," said Betty gently, "I know what's on your mind. You're worried about your pension. It's much easier to have me a guilty suicide than here alive. You're afraid I'm going to make trouble for you. You're right. I am. I intend to sue the Mediterranean Line for enough money to buy the *Garda*."

The captain shrugged. "First you must prove what you say."

Betty laughed. "Do you think I jumped in the ocean of my own free will?"

"Stranger things have happened."

"Oh, come now," said Lieutenant Colby shortly. "Nothing quite that strange."

The captain said grudgingly, "It is only a possibility, no more."

Lieutenant Colby said, "I think we'll ask Mr. Finsch some questions. Perhaps we had better move to the mess-hall. We're rather crowded in here."

In the mess-hall Betty took a seat back against the bulkhead with Lionel Haworth beside her. The captain sat in his usual place. Lieutenant Colby and the plain-clothes man remained standing. The steward went to summon Mik Finsch.

There was silence. Something in the quality of the waiting told Betty that no one, not even the captain, any longer had doubts about the case.

There were footsteps. Mik Finsch entered the mess-hall. He was wearing his light gray suit, with a yellow sport shirt. He looked amiably around the room, nodding to the captain. His eyes fell on Betty. He stiffened, stared. No one spoke. Finsch darted a glance around the room. Everyone was watching him. His amiability was gone. He spoke in a voice which rang hollow and brassy. "What has she been saying?"

"She says you're a murderer," Lieutenant Colby told him.

"That is a lie. She is the murderer. She jumped in the water because she could not face the consequence."

Betty smiled wanly.

Finsch drew a deep breath. "She is a skillful liar. Believe nothing of what she says. I have been a policeman, I know much of liars. I can prove what I say. I can prove she stole my gun, that she shot Alan Calder."

"I can prove I didn't," said Betty.

"That is impossible!"

"Just a moment," said Lieutenant Colby. "Let's proceed with a certain degree of order. All this is very interesting. What is this proof you speak of?"

"I will show you," said Finsch. "I must go to my cabin."

"I must go to my cabin too," said Betty. "I'll show you my proof."

# 3

Five minutes later Betty, with the plain-clothes man who had accompanied her, returned to the mess-hall. She had changed into her blue jeans, her white polo shirt, and she carried her small white purse.

Finsch already had returned and stood by the table with his green jade ball on a handkerchief in front of him. He was talking volubly to Colby, pointing out the fingerprints on the jade.

"Those are my fingerprints," said Betty. "I admit it. I put them there after Alan Calder was shot."

"So you say," sneered Finsch. "Where is your proof?"

"Look at me. I'm the proof. These are the clothes I wore ashore. I rode on the launch with the Catos, with Harry Mayberry and Nello. Where did I carry the gun?"

No one answered; there was no need. The jeans clung to her like a second skin. The polo shirt could hardly have concealed a button. Her purse was barely large enough to hold her lipstick and a wallet.

"Nello took pictures," said Betty. "The film is in his camera."

Finsch reached for his jade ball, the muscles on his face twisted into ropes. He threw the ball with tremendous force. Betty ducked. The jade struck the wall beside her, shattered.

Finsch had already started for the door. "Just a minute, Mr. Finsch," said Lieutenant Colby.

Finsch ignored him. The plain-clothes man moved in front of him. "Stop, Mr. Finsch."

"You may try to stop me," said Finsch.

# 4

Betty and Lionel Haworth sat in the bar of the Panama Hotel drinking sidecars. He held her hand; she was staring into the glass, seeing far far away.

"Come now," said Lionel. "Past is past."

"I know. But I won't be myself for a long time. Maybe never."

"Who will you be?"

"Oh, you know what I mean! When I think back…"

"Don't think back. Think of now."

"I'd like to. But I can't. I feel all unsettled."

Lionel rubbed the bruise on his cheek where Finsch's fist had struck—no one had escaped unscathed. "I hate to see you leave."

"I'll be here a week. The Mediterranean Line is being very nice to me—first class passage to Italy on the *Fiesole*, first class passage home whenever I want, expenses here at the hotel."

"They prefer that you don't sue."

Betty laughed. "Captain Frascatore can keep his pension. But I'd like to pull his nose." She yawned. "Oh well…"

"For two cents," said Lionel, "I'd come to Europe with you."

Betty patted his hand. "Don't be rash, Lionel. Remember Camp Number Six."

"Camp Number Six can slide into the lake."

Betty twirled the glass, looking into the swirling amber; then she shrugged. "I must stop brooding." She drank, put down the glass, kissed Lionel on the cheek. "And now I'm going to bed. I'm very tired, I was up all last night."

They stood up. "And when will I see you again?" asked Lionel.

"As soon as you like."

"Tomorrow?"

"Tomorrow. Goodnight."

"Goodnight."

Betty went to her room. Alone, she felt uneasy, vaguely frightened. Ridiculous, she thought. I've got to get over this. She undressed, lay down on the bed. Of course I'm happy, she told herself. I'm alive!… Tears flooded her eyes. She lay crying for many minutes into her pillow.

The telephone rang. It was Lionel. "I wanted to make sure everything was all right."

"Yes, Lionel." If she weren't so tired… But no. Do be sensible, Betty. "I'm perfectly splendid."

"Don't fret."

"No. Goodnight, Lionel."

"Goodnight."

She turned off the light and presently fell asleep.

JACK VANCE was born in 1916 to a well-off California family that, as his childhood ended, fell upon hard times. As a young man he worked at a series of unsatisfying jobs before studying mining engineering, physics, journalism and English at the University of California Berkeley. Leaving school as America was going to war, he found a place as an ordinary seaman in the merchant marine. Later he worked as a rigger, surveyor, ceramicist, and carpenter before his steady production of sf, mystery novels, and short stories established him as a full-time writer.

His output over more than sixty years was prodigious and won him three Hugo Awards, a Nebula Award, a World Fantasy Award for lifetime achievement, as well as an Edgar from the Mystery Writers of America. The Science Fiction and Fantasy Writers of America named him a grandmaster and he was inducted into the Science Fiction Hall of Fame.

His works crossed genre boundaries, from dark fantasies (including the highly influential *Dying Earth* cycle of novels) to interstellar space operas, from heroic fantasy (the *Lyonesse* trilogy) to murder mysteries featuring a sheriff (the Joe Bain novels) in a rural California county. A Vance story often centered on a competent male protagonist thrust into a dangerous, evolving situation on a planet where adventure was his daily fare, or featured a young person setting out on a perilous odyssey over difficult terrain populated by entrenched, scheming enemies.

Late in his life, a world-spanning assemblage of Vance aficionados came together to return his works to their original form, restoring material cut by editors whose chief preoccupation was the page count of a pulp magazine. The result was the complete and authoritative *Vance Integral Edition* in 44 hardcover volumes. Spatterlight Press is now publishing the VIE texts as ebooks, and as print-on-demand paperbacks.

# Colophon

This book was printed using Adobe Arno Pro as the primary text font, with NeutraFace used on the cover.

This title was created from the digital archive of the Vance Integral Edition, a series of 44 books produced under the aegis of the author by a worldwide group of his readers. The VIE project gratefully acknowledges the editorial guidance of Norma Vance, as well as the cooperation of the Department of Special Collections at Boston University, whose John Holbrook Vance collection has been an important source of textual evidence.

Special thanks to R.C. Lacovara, Patrick Dusoulier, Koen Vyverman, Paul Rhoads, Chuck King, Gregory Hansen, Suan Yong, and Josh Geller for their invaluable assistance preparing final versions of the source files.

Source: Alun Hughes, Paul Rhoads, Tim Stretton, Koen Vyverman, Harrison Watson, Jr.; Digitize: Richard Chandler, Rob Friefeld, John A. Schwab; Diff: David A. Kennedy, Hans van der Veeke; Tech Proof: Koen Vyverman; Text Integrity: Patrick Dusoulier, Steve Sherman, Koen Vyverman; Implement: Donna Adams, Hans van der Veeke; Security: Tim Stretton; Compose: Andreas Irle; Comp Review: Christian J. Corley, Marcel van Genderen, Brian Gharst, Charles King, Paul Rhoads, Robin L. Rouch; Update Verify: Rob Friefeld, Marcel van Genderen, Paul Rhoads, Robin L. Rouch; RTF-Diff: Patrick Dusoulier; Textport: Patrick Dusoulier; Proofread: Neil Anderson, Michel Bazin, Mark Bradford, Antonio Duarte III, Rob Gerrand, Evert Jan de Groot, Lucie Jones, A. G. Kimlin, Robert Melson, Steve Sherman

Artwork (maps based on original drawings by Jack and Norma Vance):

Paul Rhoads, Christopher Wood

Book Composition and Typesetting: Joel Anderson

Art Direction and Cover Design: Howard Kistler

Proofing: Steve Sherman, Dave Worden

Jacket Blurb: John Vance

Management: John Vance, Koen Vyverman